ERWIN MORTIER (born 1965) made his mark in 1999 with his debut novel *Marcel*, which was awarded several prizes in Belgium and the Netherlands, and received acclaim throughout Europe. In the following years he quickly built up a reputation as one of the leading authors of his generation. His novel *While the Gods Were Sleeping* received the AKO Literature Prize, one of the most prestigious awards in the Netherlands. His latest work, *Stammered Songbook*, a raw yet tender elegy about illness and loss, was met with unanimous praise. Mortier's evocative descriptions bring past worlds brilliantly to life.

ERWIN MORTIER

SHUTTERSPEED

Translated from the Dutch by
Ina Rilke

PUSHKIN PRESS
LONDON

Pushkin Press
71–75 Shelton Street, London WC2H 9JQ

Shutterspeed first published in Dutch as *Sluitertijd* by Cossee in 2002

This translation first published in 2007 by Harvill Secker
First published by Pushkin Press in 2014

0 0 1

ISBN 978 1 782270 20 1

Offset by Tetragon, London

Printed and bound by
CPI Group (UK) Ltd., Croydon CRO 4YY

www.pushkinpress.com

SHUTTERSPEED

I STILL HAVE PHOTOS FROM THOSE DAYS, SHOWING ME fair-haired and sandal-shod. My father holds me by the hand as we stroll along meadows dappled by the shade of poplars, during summers that now seem greener and slower than they were. By the wayside, at the foot of the railway embankment, on the rise to the bridge, my father startles butterflies on the flowering hemlock, and their motion, like my wonderment, is arrested in mid-air.

This is the timelessness of the world when he was still around and I had barely arrived. For all that I am there in the picture with my eyes riveted on the pebbly road, doubtless to avoid losing my footing, and for all that I cling so tightly to his hand, my existence has yet to begin.

I must be about two years old, and it is probably August. The sights around me are finite and warm. From end to end the horizon is serrated by lines of trees cropping the surfeit of sky. Everything about their meandering boughs suggests regularity. A train passing each hour. The stroke of a bell every fifteen minutes, high in the echo chamber above the roof tiles.

By the paling around the rectory I see walnuts dropping from overhanging branches, splitting open like skulls on the cobbles. After sundown sparrows swoop around the house in search of spiders lurking in the crannies of weathered grouting. The upstairs windows are open, with net curtains that hang motionless behind the screens. Up there, over one of the display windows flanking the front door, is the room that is to be mine, the room that once belonged to my father and Werner, his twin brother.

The table with its single drawer, the bookshelf, the chair. Up on the mantelpiece the picture of John Kennedy, from which position it was never moved, not even by me. The cherrywood wardrobe. The grass-green bedspread. The pre-war lino, fractured between feet and floorboard. The bed, which they must have shared like two sardines in a tin when they were boys, and which started out too big for me just as it did for them, and then became too small.

Two glass-fronted shop counters on the ground floor, then a doorway to a long passage leading to the back of the house. From the ceiling dangle the legs of almost life-size dolls, looking like hanged men in clear plastic bags, side by side with bicycle wheels, pitchers and fly swatters.

Daylight filters darkly through the cluttered window displays into the shop, where shelves and storage cabinets with drawers stretch from floor to ceiling. Racks of bottles and jars, some of them filmed with dust; rows of liqueurs from godforsaken times, tiers of brightly coloured pill-boxes — the salves and potions of Uncle Werner's sideline in dubious remedies for every conceivable ailment. Hanging gardens of tinned pineapple, apricot and peach teeter on the brinks of precipices. Further back, like treasure-hunters' bounty, gleam glacé cherries in tall glass jars. A glass showcase, fitted with a lock by Aunt Laura, Uncle Werner's wife, holds a polar region of crystal bottles and phials of essential oils, so ethereal and precious that they are almost sold by the drop.

The shop-front is still recognisable. You can tell from the size of the windows that they were once used for display, but the walls are no more than a shell; the house itself has moved elsewhere. The inside doors now open on to rooms in other remembered houses, leading from one to the other in seamless transition.

Dates are irrelevant. One moment I am standing with my feet in a zinc tub, twisting round to peer at my buttocks in the mirror, the next I have just been lifted from my cradle and am being wrapped in a blanket by a woman.

There are also spaces without walls, only the chequered pattern of a tiled floor strewn with jigsaw pieces. I can feel the cold tiles beneath my feet, I can hear whispers that sound as if they are coming from a tube somewhere in the passage behind me. I am far too young to understand what they are saying, but I have a sense of voices being lowered on account of me being here and my father having gone.

Coming home after work on a Friday night he would

have sweets hidden in his fists, or else disappointment. He was never empty-handed.

I can see them now, the fists of a manual worker, thick fingers, coarse dark hairs on the wrists, and the palms so hard-callused as to give the impression of stone or some other lifeless, carved material.

All the rest, the dark hair that was almost as dark as mine is now, the thick lashes, the eyes set deep in their sockets, are things I am not sure if I remember or am just imagining. The fists, though, I am sure about.

He was a little sturdier than his twin brother. Broader shoulders, bigger bones. Their mother always said he had stayed inside her the longest and had kicked Werner out first, and that she had had to stop him from sucking both her breasts dry.

In a garden of long ago she sits on a chair, wide-kneed, still dazed from giving birth, her infant sons like small Buddhas on her lap. Uncle Werner looks at once earnest and unconcerned, while my father's gaze seems turned inward, or just vacant. Sated, full, the pair of them.

On the day of their baptism my father sleeps through the whole ceremony, a small bundle of newbornness in white lace. Even as the priest pours water on his forehead from a brass shell, he does not stir.

At the festivities afterwards he and his twin lie forehead to forehead in a wicker cradle festooned with lilies: fists bunched, eyes shut tight, knees drawn up against bellies, as though still resisting the dread passage from womb to world.

Beneath his eyelids the pupils twitch to the rhythm of unsteady dreams. In his oversized head his spirit must already be branching out into all those brain cells.

His fingers grasp at everything and nothing. When someone strokes his cheek, so gratuitously veined with life, his face reciprocates with a wide grimace which he has yet to learn is a smile and connected with pleasure.

They were inseparable. Forever side by side, identically dressed, posing in relatives' gardens, where he trailed after his twin among the flowerbeds, apparently without ever getting his clothes dirty.

He always seems to freeze in a self-conscious pose, hands on the stomach, face slightly averted, with that narrow-eyed look of his that shoots past me as if to say: 'Don't touch, don't look, let me be. I'm not here.'

The sight of me wearing the same strained expression at the age of about twelve, here, in the doorway of the shop on a Sunday in late May, still gives me the vertigo of someone posing on a cliff edge.

It is the day of my First Communion. The shop is closed. Aunt Laura has hung sheets across the bottom half of the display windows, because her wares need protection from the summer glare, unlike us, for whom the spiked morning sunlight holds no menace.

There are three of us standing on the doorstep, huddled together as if there isn't enough room for us all in the picture. I wear grey knee breeches and a tartan blazer over a shirt with a bow tie, my cheeks still on fire after Aunt's harsh scouring. Uncle Werner wears his usual kindly, slightly loopy grin as he rests his hand on my shoulder, looking down at me as if he were my real father.

My lips are curved into a smile that has clearly been cajoled out of me. My sweaty, satin-gloved hands clasp a soft leather-bound missal with gilt-edged pages and a string of rosary beads.

I am visibly embarrassed by my knee socks and my sissy appearance in general.

Emerging from the church afterwards, standing on the steps amid hats and collars, partially screened by Aunt's coat swinging open as she raises her arm to steady her hat for no good reason, I offer the same dutiful smile, but my eyes are guarded, as if I had only just noticed the photographer focusing on me and had braced myself in the nick of time for the all-seeing lens.

I look straight into the camera, my face like a raised fist against the dark background of the portal. In the way I have quickly struck a pose, one foot slightly in front of the other, left hand on my hip and the right in my trouser pocket, I recognise the wish to resemble my father and fill his frame with my own.

I wanted to feel what he had felt, to feel it tingle in my own pores on the very same spot where he once posed for the camera, bathed in an equally summery sunshine which, over the years, turned his complexion sallow. He wore a similar blazer, only speckled. His shirt, tie and shoes look old and worn in the photo.

It was taken just after the war, so perhaps only the jacket was new.

At the post-Communion party I am the centre of attention: a grave-looking boy occupying the place of honour beneath the mantelpiece in the invariably stuffy front room. I am delivering the *coup de grâce* to the lamb-shaped frozen dessert, apparently oblivious to all those bored elbows propped on the table.

Displayed on the sideboard at my back is the candle Aunt Laura bought for me, inscribed with my name, Joris Alderweireldt, in gilt lettering beneath a Lamb of God holding a crucifix in its front paws.

Later, when the table has been cleared, I unwrap the parcel Uncle Werner deposited on the sideboard in the morning with a conspiratorial air, saying it was not to be opened until later. I do my best to look surprised and pleased as the wrapping paper parts to reveal a black case containing a hefty pair of binoculars, smelling of new.

There I am, reaching inside the case for a narrow envelope wedged in the bottom. I remember my heart leaping then sinking at the sight of the familiar hand, a neat copperplate with a hint of the schoolgirl disciplined by years of ruler-wielding nuns.

The heading would have been the usual 'My darling boy'. Perhaps I was too young, perhaps not, to get a sense of the stiltedness, the hesitation before putting pen to paper, possibly even a smattering of guilt or remorse sweepingly glossed over by how much she missed being with me today, and did I like the Spanish stamps. Spain, land of tangerines and St Nicholas, who showed considerably less reluctance than her to board a boat or train.

Aunt leans back in her chair, giving one of the wry smiles she reserves for signalling disapproval. There is a hint of unease in the faces around her, whereas I look quite serene, and it is only now that I realise how much energy it cost me to hold up the letter, which was more like an oversized postcard, as if I am going to read it aloud.

Over the scene hangs a pall of silence, shot through with the painfully measured ticking of the mantel clock. Twenty minutes to three. Outside, the hens have settled in their dusty hollows, over in the churchyard the gravestones are blistering in the heat.

There is no one 'from her side', as Aunt used to call my mother's relations. They must have lost touch over time. There are a few photos, not many, in which one of her brothers is to be seen: a man with a pointed moustache and dark glasses, his teeth bared in a forced smile that seems all the grimmer for the glint of gold fillings, while I blow out candles or skip around a Christmas tree.

He has her lean build, her long fingers, and a vulnerable agility which, here on this camping holiday on the moors, does not tally with how I remember him. I am sitting in the long grass at his feet playing with a bucket, while he looks out over the car towards the tent and the figure of a woman picking daisies on a rise farther off.

The various homes belonging to members of her family are intertwined in my memory to form a single labyrinthine building with a different season at each window. The straight-edged lawns, the well-trodden paths, the chicken runs edged with elder have all come together in one vast garden of secret walks and terraces shaded by spreading branches. Beyond the trees rise the house-tops, cool, stately, aloof, darkened with soot or rain, as if the brickwork were steeped in its own shadow.

My mother looms palely in dim interiors filled with massive furniture, a blond toddler at her knee, her brothers forming a defensive rampart around her. At the age of eighteen, in the company of some relatives – on her birthday, perhaps – there is no sign of the rebellious spirit she must have possessed for her to invoke her clan's contempt by marrying beneath her. I see a young girl, frail and prim in a jacket and skirt, her hair up, blinking against the harsh afternoon sunshine as she poses among overblown peonies on a lawn, two pigeons like snowy napkins in the grass at her feet.

She stands among the tables laden with refreshments, partially obscured by summer hats, shoulders, politely smiling faces and hands arrested in mid-gesture, and chats with her friends – ladies in the making with handbags and summer gloves they would prefer to keep on when shaking hands with gentlemen. She is a Nachtergaele, a name that resonates in the village. There is no trace of the awkwardness I feel every time a camera is pointed at me, the same awkwardness as my father's and which always makes me, like him, look like a photo within a photo hanging crookedly on a wall in the final moment before it shatters to pieces on the floor.

At a fairground dance she sails across the floor in the arms of one of her brothers. On another occasion she claps her hands for the boys' sack race on the lawn. A fine-tuned mechanism of civilities and platitudes governs her gestures in these snapshots, tempering her response to jests by removing their sting.

On an outing, beneath the cherry blossom, surrounded by her beaming girlfriends, she winks coyly at the camera as she raises a foaming tankard to her lips. At the same instant a man at the next table – my father, as it turns out – beckons a waitress, leaning so far back that his head almost touches her ear. They seem utterly unaware of one another.

Somebody snapped the pair of them in a field of ripe corn, peering happily over the swollen ears. That summer the fathomless sky was a shade of blue that only the earliest colour photographs were able to record. Studio-enhanced, no doubt.

Later, they hold hands as they gaze over a mountain lake, two unassuming silhouettes standing at the edge of a glassy stretch of water encircled by steep cliffs and snow-capped peaks. He carries a rucksack, she leans on a walking stick. The light has an icy clarity, making them seem almost as transparent as the feathery clouds high over their heads, swirling around the mountain-tops.

One winter's day he sits on his heels on a frosted

football pitch, his arms around his mates' shoulders. Judging by the twinkle in his eye it must have been her taking the picture. She seems to have had some trouble focusing the lens; perhaps the sight of him with tousled hair, unbuttoned shirt, and thighs glistening with post-match sweat made her head spin.

How he must have loved her wide skirts, her sleeveless blouses showing off her pretty arms. He lifts her over puddles, thresholds, ditches, just for the fun of encircling her small waist with his hands.

The long pigtail that tied her to her girlhood has suddenly gone. Her hair is short and bouncy, with curls flying in jubilation at their newfound freedom after so many years of constraint, or perhaps it was just that she thought the new hairstyle went well with the wedding band on her finger.

In a meadow on the outskirts of the village she sits on a rug under a greening willow, holding herself with the propriety she must have acquired through careful instruction. The slightly strained elegance of knees and ankles kept close together makes her look older than her years. Her hand reaches out to my father, from whose vantage I observe her now, showing him something, a blade of grass or a twig perhaps, and apparently speaking to him.

Here she repeats the same gesture. At a table set up in the garden she offers my father a spoonful of jam to taste, cupping his chin with her free hand. He cranes his neck, mouth agape. She holds the spoon just beyond his reach.

There is no sign of me anywhere. But the fruit trees behind them look familiar. The white-washed trunks are a little thinner than I remember, but I can tell by their leafy crowns and the deep shadows on the grass that June is drawing to a close. They must have been picking cherries. In the scullery there would have been a pan on the boil, and steaming jars lined up on the draining board.

It is their last summer without me. She is as round as a cannonball. Her breasts loll like mounds of fat on her midriff. Her arms are strewn with freckles, as if inside the batik tent-dress she were succumbing to the never-ending thirst with which I am sapping her lifeblood.

I must have dug my heels into her stomach, butted my head against her bladder, sent her running to the kitchen pump day and night to gulp down water in an effort to dull the vicarious craving for sugar, pickled herring or raw milk, made her want to purge her flesh of me, who was plundering her like a larder.

With an expression of wonder, which with hindsight qualifies as maternal love, she gazes at the white bundle in her arms. My father sits on the side of the bed, leaning over to run a fingertip over my brow. He seems afraid to touch me — me, half of him, but more inextricably entwined with her than he has ever been.

In the chapel at the hospital he watches impassively as Uncle Werner lights the baptismal candle while their mother, wasted by the disease that will soon kill her, holds me over the font. She looks uncertain, almost as if I could slip from her hands any moment. In the next picture my father, having taken me from her arms, pulls funny faces in the hope of quieting my howls.

I cannot possibly remember any of it, and yet I can see his face before me, vague and ethereal like the marbled rainbow stripes on the lenses of my binoculars.

On the evening after my First Communion, while the sky clouded over, I stood by the open window in my bedroom and unscrewed the caps on the lenses. Aunt was downstairs doing the dishes, Uncle Werner was feeding the hens in the back yard.

It took me a while to work out how to adjust the focus so that the church appeared in minute detail. I could distinguish the hairline cracks in the rendering on the spire, just as I could count the leaves of the linden tree in the road, pale green against the darkening sky.

I told myself there must be a world out there stocked with all the images that had never been captured, except by the sunshine perhaps, which always seemed to absorb a smattering of whatever it illuminated, reuniting it God knows where with all those two-dimensional figures patiently prised from frames, albums or the depths of the old suitcase in which I kept my most treasured possessions.

I waited until it was nearly dark before dragging the case out from under the bed, raising the lid and adding my mother's letter to the others inside.

The coppery sheen of the sun sinking behind the trees that evening conjured a vast, shimmering lake or reservoir, an afterlife of once reflected surfaces, fragile and inaccessible.

I see the same light, but much longer ago. In a room somewhere I hear footsteps, a door swings open on squealing hinges and someone calls my name.

Try as I may, I cannot pull myself upright. I feel anger welling up inside me, the briny prickle of tears in my eyes.

I remember my shoes: blue with leather laces. I can still hear the sound they made on the tiles when I flew into a rage and kicked all my cars, building blocks and pencils across the room.

I see my father reaching out to me. There is something about his broad grin that makes my mother's soft features seem surprisingly stern at times.

Hanging on to his fingers to pull myself up, I almost lose my balance, and a tingling sensation shoots down my shins.

In some pantry or kitchen at the back, a leaky tap drips on to the lid of a saucepan, and the echo rings with the emptiness of the whole house.

My father lifts me, makes the wind whistle in my blond hair and throws me up in the air, higher and higher. My chest tightens. I hear myself shriek more in terror than in mirth as my body leaves his hands and I grow conscious of being surrounded by air.

He probably cried something like 'Up you go, Joris! Fly!' But his lips offer no clues.

I do not know who took that picture, who it was that left me suspended for ever in mid-air above my father's splayed fingers, like an alarmed putto in a painting.

OF THAT LAST SUMMER I HAVE ONLY A FEW DISTINCT memories. In the unrelenting heat of those months the days seemed to run together into a single, long day, as though intent on confirming Aunt's prediction that this would be the last of the good life for me. The world was immersed from May to late August in the shimmer of a dream, deep beneath the surface of sleep. I was eleven and had learned about Newton. I could write and spell, I could read the hands of the clock and work out what time it was outdoors, where the hours made a difference.

The day the photographer came to take the annual class photo our master, Mr Snellaert, turned up at school wearing his best suit and his homburg with a jaunty blue feather tucked in the headband.

He lined us up four rows deep in the playground, in the shadow cast by the arcade. July was already weighing down the trees. The end of term was drawing near, and I was feeling the hypnotic approach of the summer holidays.

'I shall count up to five,' said the master. 'At three you keep still, and at five we'll be done.'

He snapped his fingers and we held our breath. A dry click sounded and the next thing we knew it was all over.

I wore the beige nylon shirt Aunt Laura had quickly ferreted out from the top shelves in the shop, where skeins of knitting wool awaited the cold season like eternal snow. The fabric chafed my arms and chest and irritated the skin of my neck. The stubborn smell of plastic packaging and cardboard collar-strip lingered in the seams all day long.

I felt strangely crease-proof, starched, new, and when we filed back to the classroom Mr Snellaert growled: 'Alderweireldt, boy, you gave your usual impression of an ironing board, that's for sure.'

He always had me in his sights. There were times that I suddenly felt the weight of his eyes, his latent sarcasm impinging on me like a fly on my forearm when I was busy lining up my ruler exactly parallel to the side of my desk, or couldn't decide where to lay my jotter – underneath or beside my reading book – or how to position my protractor or my pencils, but most of all when for the umpteenth time I frantically crossed out the opening line of my composition, shielding the page with my left arm for fear that the words I needed would evaporate before I had a chance to commit their sounds to paper.

Just as unexpectedly he would lay a heavy hand on my shoulder, as if he had crept up on me, soundlessly treading on the tiled floor in which his soles had worn out a shiny path.

'Eyes like marbles and still you don't know where to look,' he said, pushing my head down over my desk.

His fingers seemed to be kneading the muscles around my bones, massaging my spine to make it longer, and shaking my head so that the thoughts, which were like as not lost in the branches of the apple tree by the big window, fell from my hair like unripe fruit.

'Get on with it. Too finicky by half, you are . . .'

The boys squirmed in their seats, nudging and smirking, but it could also happen that their gales of laughter descended on me like a hailstorm, especially when the master went round collecting up the exercise books while I was still labouring to end what I had scarcely begun, my handwriting chasing over the lines in an ever wilder scrawl.

'You'll be late for the Last Judgment at this rate. And what'll you do then, eh?' he sneered. 'Hang around in space? Or put your hand up and moan: Oh sir, wait sir, I'm not ready yet, sir!'

The ensuing jeers and sniggers moved me to retreat into more or less wounded silence, and to fix my gaze on the dark green dust coat which he donned morning and afternoon as if it were his robe of office.

Back in the days when my father and Uncle Werner were his pupils, his hair had been dark and wavy and his paunch nowhere near sagging.

The annual school photo was not taken in the playground then, but indoors, with all the boys at their desks and the master standing right at the back of the classroom, ramrod-stiff in the space between the stove and the row my father was in. He sat near the window, shoulders hunched and arms folded, as if none of it had anything to do with him.

Perhaps it took longer then to adjust the camera, a redoubtable contraption that reminded me of a cannon, what with the blinding flash and the loud crack as it fired into the air to startle my father. He is not sitting bolt upright but inclining his frame slightly, away from the master and towards the window. On the ledge close to his elbow the potted geraniums crane towards the glass, making all their veins show up against the chill spring light.

Some of the maps hanging on the wall above the cupboards are familiar. Perhaps, in the bleakness of morning lessons, he stared as long and hard as I did at the continents, so that their shapes would perform a shadow dance across the retina when we shut our eyes tight. Perhaps he was just as relieved as I was to come down to earth when the master rummaged in those same cupboards to prepare the next initiation of his boys into the secrets of the Natural World.

On days of particularly gruelling sums, when our toil was deemed worthy of reward, the master went over to the cupboard at the back of the classroom and brought out the model of the solar system. He set it up on his desk and called us all to come forward, and once we were crowding round he would, as often as not, take a deep breath and blow the dust off Saturn's rings into our faces before making the moon turn around the earth in front of our astonished eyes, and the earth around the sun along with all the planets.

'In the heavens above,' he intoned, 'everything runs like clockwork.'

If we were good we were allowed to take turns at the handle, making the time-warped copper filaments vibrate as they moved the heavenly bodies in circles around an old light bulb, accelerating the years to mere seconds.

It was not until I turned the handle the wrong way, less accidentally than I made out, thereby bringing the entire mechanism to a halt, that the master lost his patience. 'Ah, you again. I might have known.'

He had all the answers, but that didn't mean I always took him at his word. Later that day, when he filled a kettle with water before our eyes and put it on a burner until the spout emitted a ribbon of steam, thus proving to his boys that of all matter it was only the form that changed, I did not believe him.

Where did that leave the gestures I made when shifting in my seat, stretching out in my chair, crossing my ankles, or spreading my arms and splaying my fingers on my desk?

When the master let the steam condense against a sheet of glass and caught the drops of moisture in a cup, the sunlight seemed to loosen me up and rarefy my thoughts. If I had shut my eyes then, I would have seen myself sliding from my desk like a sheet of paper, zigzagging into blissful, stultifying sleep.

There were weeks when I suppressed my truculence to act the paragon of virtue, paying slavish attention to the master, readily accepting the role of goody-goody. When commended I lowered my eyes modestly and relished the exquisite self-loathing brought on by the pride flushing my cheeks.

There were also times when I stopped washing my hair and didn't change my underwear until it was unspeakably filthy, so that I could sniff my whole crusty body from under the clean shirt I wore on top.

I would vegetate for hours, lying back on my bed with my legs flung wide, or lolling against a wall, as lazy as the neighbour's flea-ridden dog on the pavement outside. If Aunt called my name or Uncle knocked on my door, I curled my lip and saw myself baring my teeth in the shiny varnish of the headboard.

I longed to be as dishevelled as the drawers of my wardrobe, which I deliberately left half open with a pair of underpants or a sock draped over the side. I longed to be as spineless as my satchel when I let it drop from my hands after school and kicked it against the leg of my writing table.

I dawdled over the drawings in my jotter, tracing the outlines of kingdoms shaped like ink blots or paint splashes, using crayons to mark them with roads in different colours, the more hairpin bends the better, and with mountain ranges so high that I gasped for air above the snow-line.

I gave my countries names more exotic even than Ouagadougou or Agadir. I drew trading ships in the harbours and sent the cargoes over complicated railway networks to the most remote regions. Each country was an island, like me, surrounded by an ocean with narrow fjords penetrating deep into my heartland.

I also drew forgotten kingdoms, undiscovered by any explorer and inhabited by people who had no idea where they were. Boundless, imaginary lands, where each moment of the day was private and secret, as were my own thoughts in after-school hours, when the master's spell was broken and things became weightless.

When I got home that afternoon Aunt Laura told me to take off my clean shirt; I would only get it dirty, and anyway it was too hot.

She was shelling peas at the table under the cherry tree in the back garden. With the routine precision that characterised all her gestures, she dug her thumb into the tough pods and pushed the peas to the end until they dropped like stillborn babes into an enamel basin on her lap.

She was economical in every way. 'We're not rolling in it, but we get by,' she would say with proud resignation.

The compactness of her frame gave her the appearance of being in control, but her composure could be demolished from one moment to the next by a nervous tic in her right eyelid, which sometimes caused her to start winking at me or at Uncle or at customers in the shop, which widowers and bachelors in particular found unsettling.

She went through all the motions of being my mother,

laying an arm around my shoulder from time to time or ruffling my hair, but she was too bony and too short to convince me.

'I hope you smiled for once in your life,' she said without looking up from her work. 'In every picture up to now you look as miserable as a nun at a funeral.'

She thought it a waste of money. On the dresser in the back room I was already present in five school photos amid classmates and master, with a face like sour milk, as Uncle Werner used to say.

'Now, your dad,' Aunt Laura went on, 'he was serious, just like you. That look of his, as if he had a stack of tax forms to fill in . . . As for you, you ought to spend more time with your friends, and if that doesn't appeal, there's plenty of work to be done around here, plenty of chores to occupy idle hands.'

I knew she liked it when I broke in with a loud, plaintive 'Ma!' in mock protest. Our tokens of affection were offered at exchange rates only she and I were privy to. Neither of us was good at compliments. We dressed them up in rags of ill-temper.

'The padre caught you fooling around in the graveyard again,' she said, sweeping the empty pods into a bucket. 'What will people think, Joris? I wish you'd behave. You'll knock a corner off your father's gravestone if you're not careful. And that would be expensive to repair, you know.'

My father lay by the western wall, a few paces from the shop, under a slab of unpolished Belgian bluestone which always left my hands white with dust when I ran them

23

over the rough-hewn edges. On hot afternoons I sometimes smeared a gob of spittle on the slab and watched
the stain dwindle rapidly in the sunshine. Walking home
from school I would show off to my friends by skipping
down the gravelled paths between the graves, chanting
the names on the headstones to the tune of nursery songs,
and I would make a point of slipping my father's name in
among the rest without anyone noticing. I tucked him up
and sang him lullabies, leaving him to turn over each time
the church bell struck the hour while he carried on
sleeping and dwindling.

Dying might be a bit like evaporating, dissipating into
the afternoon, succumbing to the soporific scrabble of
pigeons in the guttering on the roof, and heaven was the
place where the souls of the dead condensed on God's
cold countenance and ran like tears down His cheeks into
His cupped palm.

In the classroom Death carried a scythe over his
shoulder and turned an hourglass. His face was obscured
by a pitch-black cloak, with 'Time flies, use it wisely!'
written across it in flaming letters, but each time the classroom door swung shut he fluttered so frivolously on the
pin holding him to the noticeboard that I couldn't take
him too seriously.

He ought to have merely swayed in a noble sort of way,
with the slow grace of seaweed rippling on the tide, ruling
over a domain where nothing moved of its own accord,
rather like the beetles I kept in jars at home, who bided
their time in utter immobility. Eventually they grew so

fragile that their antennae fell off when I lifted their glass dungeon with both hands and shook it.

I tried holding my breath some days, and if I kept it up long enough I could feel something inside me drop through narrow funnels, but my midriff rebelled and drew gulps of fresh air into my lungs. When I tried closing my eyes against the light, I found myself sinking deeper and deeper into an aching tide of boredom that swelled each time the tower bell struck another quarter-hour.

I wanted to lose myself, lose a shoe, feel my socks sliding off my feet between the sheets, or my feet sliding out of my socks, and then fumble around to retrieve them, which would be in vain because they were just as lost as I was. But I was dangling like a fly in a daytime web and there was no escape.

'If you like, you can pour those lovelies into the jars,' said Aunt, reaching me the bowl with peas.

'Mind you don't spill any. Peas are in precious short supply, what with the drought these past weeks.'

I shook my head, stood up and made off towards the road, while she called after me not to be too long. I ran round the back, down the church lane between the claustrophobic beech hedges which only last month had been alive with buzzing beetles, past the tree-lined alleyway to the big house, and past the tankers pumping chilled milk into stainless-steel vats at the dairy.

I slowed my pace along the last row of cottages before

the bridge across the stream. I settled myself on the brick parapet. It was my favourite spot for doing nothing but taking in the sweet summer air, the whisper of the wind in the rushes along the bank, and the water sliding languidly beneath my feet towards the manor. Upon reaching the trees in the park, the stream branched out into countless little creeks which vanished among the trunks before coming together again in the pond by the terrace, where carp rose to the surface, snapping for air or midges in the drowsy warmth, and swans curved their necks into question marks.

In those days the world still fitted in my hand, but my hold on it was not as tight as I imagined. I saw my face reflected in the dark water, ringed by a school of sticklebacks which darted away into the weed when I swung my legs over the parapet.

I was reaching the age of standing very close to my wardrobe mirror, not to watch the glass mist up with my breath, but to butt my head against my reflection and shatter the image of myself sitting on the side of my bed, hunched over the suitcase full of postcards, letters and photos, rooting and rooting among all those dead papers with fingers itching to tear everything into tiny scraps. Not that I ever did.

The days were still circular in shape. As far as I was concerned the sun was tied to the spire with invisible string, turning around the earth, whatever Mr Snellaert or Galileo said.

I heard the church bells signalling the end of vespers.

26

Another moment or two and I would hear the women's voices in the lane and the patter of their shoes on the cobbles.

The daylight was already tinged with blue in the linden trees by the graveyard when I made my way back home. From the open door of the café across the road the smell of stale beer and the jangle of the jukebox wafted towards me. The church was closed. The stained-glass windows, which glowed crimson during the service, had reverted to blackness.

I walked down the path among the graves as solemnly as I could, fighting down the urge to hop and skip, and only quickened my step when I knew I was screened from view first by the branches of the linden trees and then by the paling around the rectory garden.

I liked the orderliness of the grand register of deaths that formed the heart of my inner world. God himself had put His flock to sleep in neat rows, like a collection of stamps in an album, postmarked with the dates of their first and last breaths. He was up in the belfry, using a magnifying glass and tweezers to feather the gunmetal craws of pigeons, which He flung into the sky by the handful each time the bells pealed.

The master said that the names of everybody who had ever lived or would ever live were written in the palm of His hand — some more smudged than others, he had added, casting a meaningful look at me.

*

27

As I pushed the door open, the tinkle of the shop's bell betrayed my presence. I glimpsed Uncle Werner at the far end of the passage, looking in my direction. He could not have seen me in the dark, but I could see him patting someone's arm, some visitor sitting beside him at the kitchen table beneath the lamp with the frosted glass shade, which was already lit. As I approached I recognised the tobacco-thickened voice of the dearly beloved leader of our flock, the venerable Father Amelinckx.

'I suppose they'll put up a notice,' I heard him say, 'but I would rather tell people myself . . .' He fell silent when I came in.

I expected a ticking off for leaving great big footprints all over the freshly raked earth between the graves, which the verger always made such a fuss about, but all he did was put out his hand and say my name.

Uncle Werner motioned me to shake the proffered hand.

'Sit yourself down,' cried Aunt, coming in from the back with a steaming pan in her hands.

I went up the stairs, across the landing, and into my bedroom. I shut the door behind me, stripped off my shirt, wadded it into a ball to mop the sweat from my chest and armpits, then dropped it on my writing table.

On evenings like this nothing was emptier than my room. The penetrating smell of the lino creaking under my feet and the dust in the flaking paint on the windowsill got into my nose, making me even more tense.

I felt like climbing the walls, somersaulting backwards,

screwing up sheets of paper, kicking everything in sight. I grabbed my school satchel and hurled it on my bed like a child having a tantrum, I gave the spiral-bound desk diary such a hard shove that the days rose up and swayed to and fro accusingly.

I slammed open the leather-bound missal Aunt gave me for my First Communion, which I always left on my table in exactly the same position just to get at her. The tissue-thin pages rippled and came to rest.

I pulled off my socks, relished the cool air around my feet and sat down.

'Joris, your food's getting cold,' Aunt called from the bottom of the stairs.

I held up the missal and, just before clapping it shut to feel the rush of air hitting my cheeks, I glimpsed the words *Thou has sent widows away empty, and the arms of the fatherless have been broken.*

THAT NIGHT THERE WAS A THUNDERSTORM.

'Doesn't look too good out there,' said Uncle. He had got up from his chair by the reading lamp and was pulling all the plugs from their sockets. Aunt continued playing Patience with stoic resignation.

'Funny, that,' she said in a peevish tone just as Uncle made to sit down again. 'Whenever you decide to disconnect the electric all over the place, you leave the lamp by your chair on. As if we're the only ones the lightning has it in for.'

He heaved an indifferent sigh, switched off his reading lamp and left the room to hunt for candles elsewhere in the house. Aunt could get rather tetchy in this kind of weather. Uncle had also turned off the radio, so that she was missing *Songs from the Homeland,* her favourite programme.

'Why don't you read me something, Joris,' she said. 'It would take my mind off the storm at least.'

A few days earlier, Mr Snellaert had given me a book to take home: *Mysteries of Nature Unravelled.* In contrast to my school reports, which he said bore a strong resemblance to the Pyrenees with all those soaring peaks and deep valleys, my love of reading met with his approval.

'What's it about?' she wanted to know.

'All sorts of things,' I said.

'So long as it's not about prehistoric monsters, it'll do for me.' She found it impossible to believe that such dreadful creatures had ever walked the earth. A spider in the bathroom was enough to scare the living daylights out of her.

'Don't worry,' I replied, and cleared my throat.

'It says here,' I intoned, 'that Palissy, an avowed Protestant, wrote a book called *A Wonderful Tale of Waters and Fountains*, in which he established, after long years of study, that each snowflake falling on the top of a mountain helps to feed the world's great rivers, and even the oceans!'

'Did he really need to do all that studying just for that?' Uncle grinned, setting a candle on the table. 'Just to find out that water always goes down, never up? If that's all it takes, I could be a professor myself . . .'

'Werner!' hissed Aunt. 'Just let the boy get on with it.'

The book contained wonderful pictures, including one in which the heavens resembled a bell jar made of crystal, or a soap bubble. Tucked away in a corner at the bottom was a little man who, having walked to the end of the earth, poked his head out through the side, apparently reaching for the stars with one hand. *The vast unknown and the foolhardiness of the human spirit*, read the inscription.

Other pages had brightly coloured illustrations with

captions like *The earth before the dawn of civilisation*, in which the continents didn't look at all like the wall maps in our classroom. As though God Himself had hesitated even as He was creating. As if He had experimented with all sorts of shapes in His rough sketches, cleaving continents in two or more pieces and drawing inordinately squiggly coastlines, and it seemed to me that He must have been trying to escape a kind of boredom that was a thousand times worse than the boredom I suffered every morning around eleven o'clock, when noon seemed aeons away.

Some places on earth, like the Pacific Ocean, looked as if He had skimmed over them in a semi-sleep, dreaming of land masses which, upon waking, He had crumbled between His fingers into a dusting of atolls.

It gave me a giddy sense of power to be able to survey the whole world and speak the names of all the deserts and mountain ranges, as if I were personally responsible for their existence. I held my hand in the light of the candle to cast a shadow on Hawaii. In my mind's eye I saw the streets of Honolulu thronged with people looking up in astonishment at the sudden eclipse of their sun. I took my magnifying glass from the table drawer and held it over the islands of Micronesia.

'All those peculiar names,' said Aunt, fretfully, 'you're not pulling my leg, are you? Houaheina, who'd ever think of it?'

She shook her head, but that was more on account of her card game not coming good yet again.

'I'm glad I was born here and not anywhere else. Not

too cold, not too hot, most of the time anyway, none of your unpronounceable names and no horrible savage beasts either. We can count our lucky stars, we can.'

She contemplated the cards she had laid out on the table for another game, placed her hands on the nape of her neck and threw back her head. The sound of the vertebrae cracking always gave me the creeps.

'Houaheina,' she mused.

Outside, the thunderstorm seemed to be waning before it had got well and truly under way. Uncle had fallen asleep; he began to snore.

'A fanfare for free,' Aunt grumbled. 'There he goes again.'

I kissed her good-night and went upstairs.

Lying naked on my bed with my feet up against the wall, I carried on reading by the light of the street lamp outside my window, which threw a luminous, silvery triangle on the sheet. I still preferred to read the way I had learned in my first year at school – not in silence but in whispers, which gave me the feeling I wasn't actually mouthing the words but fingering them carefully, as though fishing them out from the pages between thumb and forefinger.

There were words that set my teeth on edge like grit in poorly rinsed spinach, others that I swallowed whole like aspirin for fear of them tasting vile. One of my favourite words was 'iodine', which I had come across in a book called *Principles of Chemistry*. The title sounded mysteriously pleasing to my ears, if only because I was unsure what 'principles' meant.

I thought they were probably something like the shelving units we had in the shop. Principles would have their own little compartments with labels indicating names or dates, and iodine would be kept in one of them. The book said that iodine was to be found in sea water and that it occurred 'in high concentrations in the sea air', besides being 'of vital importance for proper functioning of the thyroid gland'.

I often took down the book from the ledge over my bed, just to check whether iodine was still in there, given that it was such a volatile substance, and when I read the bit about the thyroid I always felt a tickle in my throat. One day I asked Uncle Werner where that particular gland was situated. He responded by placing his thumb and fore-finger on either side of my Adam's apple and giving my throat a squeeze.

'Around there somewhere,' he said. 'In animals it's called sweetbread.' It sounded like some type of cake, but I preferred the name 'thyroid gland'. The word thyroid came from the Greek for shield, and the idea of having a shield-shaped gland in my body made me think of knights in shining armour.

At school one day, when Mr Snellaert asked whether anyone could remember what the Flemings' battle-cry had been during the Bruges uprising, when our people had at last − at long last, so he reminded us − taken up arms against the foreign invader, I jumped up from my desk without thinking and shouted 'For gland and glory!' My voice was so loud that even I was startled.

There was a long pause while the master rolled his eyes. He waited for the gales of laughter to die down, then came up to me quite calmly and gave me a resounding clip around the ear.

'What you need is a thorough drubbing,' he said in conclusion, wiping his hands on his dust coat.

After that I sometimes had the feeling that I was winding him up for the sole purpose of getting a thorough drubbing, so that I could secretly enjoy the humiliation of having my bones shaken up like an earthquake.

Words drove me mad at times. They would make the most extraordinary connections in my mind. I soaked them up like sweet-tasting poison until I was so saturated that they almost oozed from my pores. Wherever I went I left them on everything, like fingerprints.

I became so addicted that some days I woke up in a panic, not knowing where I was, groping frantically for sentences in the air like an alcoholic fumbling for the bottle in his bedside table. What a relief, after the early morning madness, to recognise the crack in the ceiling, the dingy skirting board, the pinecones on the bedposts, the green bedspread, and the chinks in the window frames out of which, in early spring, ladybirds would come crawling by the dozen after their winter sleep.

The master always used a red biro to write his niggling comments on the compositions I handed in. He thought them too high-falutin, or else too laboured. Too pompous, he said once, and the word rolled around my thoughts all day like a powder keg with a fuse. 'You spray a lone sparrow in the gutter with bullets, hoping that one of them will hit the mark,' he had said when he gave me back my composition looking like a blood-spattered bed sheet. 'You shouldn't exaggerate so.'

The others kept silent, hiding their glee. They had no idea what the teacher was on about, but I did. I was worried about making a fool of myself. There were things that sent an ecstatic shiver down my spine and made me go weak at the knees. The mere sight of the afternoon sunlight fracturing in the crown of the cherry tree outside my bedroom window was enough to set me off, or a sudden gust of wind whipping the poplars on the bank of the stream into a roar of rustling overhead, or sitting by myself in the kitchen at four-ish on a cloudless afternoon, watching a sunbeam slice through the curtains and hit the floor tiles, watching the dust dance in the light, dust particles that came from goodness knows where, from what had once been meteorites, if the master and his books were anything to go by, or from a rocky mountain ground down to humble grains of sand by the perpetual abrasion of water.

Such things made me want to shout at the top of my voice. Likewise the books in the cupboard at the back of the classroom that was unlocked only once a fortnight – I longed to shake them out like suitcases over my desk, so I might take the spilled words and hold them up to the light one by one, as if they were marbles and I had to decide which was the most beautiful, which the shiniest and which the most dulled by age.

Sometimes I found comfort in putting a perfectly round marble in my mouth, sucking its coldness and tumbling it around to make it click against my molars and then letting it roll further back, close enough to my gullet to make me gag, knowing that I should not be doing this, while on other days, when it drizzled and everything was dreary, I liked to run the tip of my tongue over an old marble that had struck the pavement countless times, just to feel some roughness, some jaggedness to relieve the monotony of perfection. And what a wonderful, mighty sensation it was to spit it out into the palm of my hand when no one was looking, wet with saliva like the chewed stone of a cherry or a peach, as if I had just gobbled up the world.

It was still hot, my eyes stung and I fought to keep them open. The light from the street lamp was too weak to see the pictures in the book properly. I could make out a ghostly figure holding a candle over what appeared to be an old man with white hair and hollow cheeks dozing in a chair.

Frederick the Great in Sanssouci on the night of his death. According to his personal physician the famous Kaiser suffered no bodily anguish upon yielding his noble soul to eternity.

Outside, a light rain had started to fall. I listened to the drops drumming dully on the leaves of the linden trees, and more loudly on the pavement.

I pushed the book away. My curiosity had evaporated into drowsiness.

I turned over on my back. The church bell sounded

half-past eleven. Downstairs, Uncle lowered the blinds. I had a sense of slowly coming apart at the seams.

Later, I was woken by a loud crash. The window screen had come loose. A blast of cold air hit my bed, raindrops spattered on my writing table.

Elsewhere in the house a door slammed, the wind howled around the windows and one thunderclap followed another in quick succession. I heard Uncle run across the landing.

Before I had well and truly come to my senses I found myself getting out of bed to shut the window. The tree-tops were being buffeted in all directions. I saw a sheet of heavy-duty plastic flapping among the gravestones, doing a cartwheel and coming to rest for a brief moment before sailing off again and catching in the branches of a tree, where it remained.

I put on my trousers and vest and went downstairs. Uncle and Aunt were both in their dressing gowns, sitting at the table while the lightning flashed through the slits in the blinds.

'Why don't you put the kettle on,' said Aunt. 'We won't have any peace for the next hour or so anyway.'

I went through to the kitchen and lit the gas under the kettle. Outside, the sky was seething with rage, the thunder was crashing everywhere.

'It's right on top of us!' I shouted.

They did not react. I took three cups from the cupboard and set out the teapot on the draining board.

I overheard Aunt saying that a vault might not be such a bad idea, though she didn't know how much it would cost.

'We must do *something*,' agreed Uncle.

I entered the room, put the cups down on the table, took teaspoons from the drawer and began to distribute them.

'Leave it,' said Aunt. 'I'll do that. Don't forget the sugar. And bring some cinnamon biscuits, will you.'

I went back to the kitchen. Out in the courtyard the rainwater gushed over the flagstones into the drain. Between two thunderclaps I heard the alarm bells go off at the level crossing.

'She never cared,' Aunt went on. 'A flowerpot once a year, that's all. She might show some interest. It's the least she could do . . .' I could hear the nervous shuffle of Uncle's slippers on the tiled floor.

The water began to boil, making the kettle whistle. I heard the scrape of a chair. 'Let's not discuss it now, Laura,' said Uncle. 'The lad . . .'

I took the kettle from the hob and filled the teapot.

We drank our tea.

'Hark at that, hark at that,' Uncle repeated after each crash of thunder. He was standing by the window, craning his neck as if he could look right through the blinds at the sky. 'Hark at that . . .'

In the meantime Aunt fished out the soggy remains of her biscuit with her teaspoon. She always left the biscuit in for far too long.

'What do we need a new vault for?' I asked as casually as I could. 'Seeing as we've got two cellars already.'

It was true. In one of them stood several empty oil drums, and in the other were endless rows of bottled fruit which had been gathering dust for years along with a stack of Aunt's unsold goods from the shop.

'What did I tell you?' said Uncle, looking hard at Aunt. He took a sip of his tea.

'Not a vault like a cellar,' said Aunt. 'It's for your uncle and me. And for your dad.'

'My dad?'

'He's got to move,' said Uncle. 'They've all got to move. Don't know why. They say it's not healthy, a churchyard in the middle of the village. They're going to make a new one, out in the fields by the lane.'

'It's only because of the Freemasons, if you ask me,' said Aunt. 'They don't like being buried in the shadow of the church. That's the reason, I'm sure. Simple as that.'

'There there, Laura,' soothed Uncle. 'There's not much we can do about it anyway.'

A loud thunderclap rattled the windows. It was as if a mighty block of ice had shattered in the air, right over the roof.

'Well that was close,' said Aunt. Shortly afterwards we heard the wail of sirens out in the street.

Uncle sat down with us again, around the table. He pushed his cup towards me.

'Our pa used to get us out of bed at night when there was a thunderstorm,' he mused as I poured him more tea.

'He'd make all three of us — our ma, your dad and me — keep watch at separate windows in case the barn was struck by lightning. We thought that was stupid. We laughed at him, and he flew into a rage. But the only time he gave us a hiding was when he caught your dad and me lying down on the bleach field during a thunderstorm so we could watch the lightning. I can still see our pa in the doorway, giving us what for. Shaking his fists, swearing and yelling for us to come inside. And we just laughed. Until the nut tree about ten metres away from us split in two with a deafening crack. We ran back to the house as fast as we could. Worst hiding I ever had in my life.'

He dipped a lump of sugar in his tea and held it between his lips to suck the sweetness.

'Dead scared, he was. You don't realise these things till later.'

The whole time he was speaking I was stirring my spoon around in my empty cup.

'Joris,' Aunt sighed, 'stop that please, it's getting on my nerves.'

'I want to go in the vault too,' I said. 'It's not fair to leave me out.'

They exchanged looks.

Uncle Werner broke the silence. 'Joris, my boy,' he said with a smile, 'whatever's got into you? No sense in you worrying your head about that, you've got a while to go yet.'

Even Aunt brightened at this. 'He's jealous,' she chortled. 'Did you hear that, Werner? The lad's jealous.'

41

'I've reason to be,' I replied gruffly, although I was close to laughing myself. 'I always have to sleep on my own, anyway.'

'Your turn will come,' said Aunt. 'Just you wait, there'll be plenty of times when you wish you could sleep alone.'

'What's that supposed to mean?' cried Uncle in feigned indignation. He leaned over the corner of the table to kiss her on the neck.

She pushed him away, giggling. 'Get off, you silly old goat.'

Then, turning to me, she smiled and ran her fingers through my hair.

For once I did not shrink away.

THE COBBLED STREET WAS STREWN WITH BROKEN BRANCHES.
Workmen disentangled a wayward sheet of plastic from a
tree near the church and swept up the fallen leaves.

Not a minute went by without the bell tinkling. It was
Saturday, the busiest day of the week, because the shop
would be closed on Monday, too.

Uncle and Aunt were run off their feet. The breakfast
table had not yet been cleared, the newspaper was spread
out among the breadcrumbs.

Aunt had left the breadbasket next to my plate, with
a clean tea towel folded over it because of the flies,
and a note for me: 'Joris, you must call at Miss van
Vooren's before 11. Like I said. Remember to comb your
hair.'

'Like I said' meant there was no point in trying to skive
off. Trifling with Miss van Vooren would not go unpun-
ished.

'Ah, Miss van Vooren,' Uncle used to say, 'a spinster if
ever there was one. Looks it too. To tell you the truth, I
have never known anyone as spinsterish as her. Sour as a
lemon, she is.'

He never made such remarks in his wife's hearing. Aunt was rather impressed by Miss van Vooren.

Miss van Vooren lived on the outskirts of the village, near the dairy and the stream. Her house was surrounded by cedars which had shot up taller than the roof over the years, and which now plunged the paths at their feet into deep shade. It was a sturdy, brick building with narrow bay windows on either side, a dilapidated south-facing veranda and, over the front door, a wrought-iron balcony that had seen better days.

Even in the freshness of that morning, the air above the garden path seemed to turn viscous as I approached the house. The sounds from the road were muffled by the trees, and the farther I walked the eerier I found the silence and the more ominous the crunch of my shoes on the gravel.

When I pressed the brass doorbell, ornate but somewhat tarnished, the tinkle took some time to die away in the hallway, suggesting spacious, gracious living quarters. Once upon a time there must have been a maid, and even a manservant according to Aunt, but the current mistress of the house had been its sole occupant for years.

It was a long while before she answered the door. Perhaps she had paused in front of the mirror above the umbrella stand to pat her hair into shape or to straighten the lapels of her slate-grey two-piece suit.

'Ah there you are, Joris,' Miss van Vooren said drily,

checking to see whether I was wiping my feet properly on the coconut doormat. 'Come in.'

She did not extend her hand. She never did. I don't know that she ever really noticed me. In her eyes I was probably little more than a glorified lackey, a shopping bag on legs, something serviceable that only merited attention when failing to respond, which did not happen often.

I followed her into the hallway. The sound of her clunky heels on the white marble floor tiles drifted up the formal staircase, which seemed all the grander for the landing with a flower arrangement from which protruded long, plumed grasses so delicate as to be pulverised at the least current of air.

A second door opened, and Miss van Vooren ushered me into the parlour. The dark wooden cabinets and crochet doilies resembling ropy cobwebs were always bathed in a muddy sort of light, as if the sunbeams, having infiltrated the room through the lace-edged net curtains, were imprisoned there, glancing from lampshade to table leg to the plates on display and back again, growing old and stale in the smell of snuff tobacco that billowed towards me each time I entered.

I found it hard to imagine that Miss van Vooren would indulge in such an eccentric habit as taking snuff. She was generally considered a beacon of rectitude and virtue, which in her case amounted to being incredibly stingy. Uncle Werner used to say she'd sooner lick the floor of the church clean with her own tongue than stump up for a floor-cloth.

Perhaps she took a pinch now and then as a kill-or-cure remedy for her chronically congested nose, a topic which, when she was feeling brighter than usual, warranted several minutes of conversation with Uncle.

For some reason he always referred to her as 'the skinny woodpecker'. But to me she was more like a dried flower in a botanical album, a flattened, faded buttercup or a poppy with vestiges of colour still in the stamens, but almost transparent and powder-dry.

Aunt pressed me to be polite to Miss van Vooren at all times. 'She's had more than her share of troubles, poor thing. You wouldn't wish it on your worst enemy, what she's been through.'

There were rumours, which seemed all the more plausible for the hushed tones in which they were passed on, that she had been jilted at the altar, that she had waited in vain at the church, where the pillars and candelabras had been decked with roses and carnations at considerable expense by her father, a man reputed to prefer sleeping with his money than his wife.

He had also paid for the crêpe de Chine gown worn by the bride, his only daughter: a shockingly expensive garment according to Aunt, though in my mind it was just as dingy and drab as the old bedspread draped over the sofa on which she now motioned me to sit. She sat down on a straight-backed chair, clasping her hands on the tabletop in front of her in a pose of authority.

'Joris, my boy,' she said, sounding unusually friendly, 'we're one bearer short for the canopy . . .'

I was baffled.

'The canopy?'

'Yes, the canopy of the heavens,' she said, 'for the procession. We are short of one bearer. Normally the eldest Dobbelaere boy does it, but he's staying with relatives down south. You're a bit young, I suppose, but on the other hand I think you're quite tall for your age, and your dad, God rest his soul, was a good bearer in his time. The priest always used to say: with an Alderweireldt on the team the heavens will be all right. What do you say, Joris, do you think you could do it?'

I hunched my shoulders. Miss van Vooren's wheedling tone put me on my guard. I had expected to be made to wait while she took a scrap of paper and made a list of what she needed from the shop. This invariably meant thinking long and hard over each item.

She would suddenly look up from her list and tell me rather sharply not to forget the tomato sauce. She always needed one tin of concentrated tomato purée, which was such a staple ingredient among all the various others – limp fillets of chicken breast, tiny portions of pale liver pâté or smidgins of low-fat cheese at which, Uncle said, even a mouse would turn up its nose – that I often simply forgot to add it to her shopping basket.

What on earth did she need it for? I pictured her sitting in the burble of the television in the evening, where, instead of having a biscuit or a slice of cake with her mug of weak tea, she would be spooning the tomato purée into her mouth straight from the tin, looking just as gleeful as I caught Aunt looking at breakfast sometimes, when she licked her finger after scraping it around a practically empty pear treacle jar.

'It's far too good, and too dear, to let it go to waste,' she would say to excuse her weakness, but that was nothing compared to Miss van Vooren's celebration of the joys of scrimping.

Miss van Vooren hoarded insufficiency. She bought minute quantities of food, regardless of type. She seemed determined to supply herself with a never-ending reservoir of disappointment, an unremitting hunger for more, and as a result of this subtle form of self-chastisement her tough, bony frame was visited by an incredible number of maladies. It was as though the different parts of her body were constantly engaged in getting their own back on the purity of her soul. But all this suffering only contributed to Miss van Vooren's complacency and pride.

There were times when she was incapable of keeping her wealth of afflictions to herself. Then she would sail into the shop, one of her famous migraines ablaze like a swarm of fireflies around the flossy hair at her temples. Everyone knew what was up immediately.

At such times she usually wore very dark sunglasses, which magically transformed her into a wasp or a horsefly. Even before she had shut the shop door behind her she would be giving stiff little waves of the hand to say that she was in no mood for any palaver.

Uncle Werner knew exactly what to do. He put on a serious face like a mask tied with elastic round his ears, leaned over the counter and enquired: 'Had a bad night then, Rosa?'

'Oooh, dreadful,' was the likely answer. If there had been a hailstorm overnight she would be sure to add: 'It was just as if I could feel the stones pelting right through my forehead.'

I was expecting her to have had one of her bad nights, spent in hellish pain as per usual, but that morning she looked remarkably brisk. She repeated her question about me helping to carry the canopy, making it sound like a great privilege.

'There is one condition, though,' she added, crinkling her cheeks: 'you have to be a virgin. I'm sure you know what I mean. But that won't be a problem, will it now?'

'I don't know,' I stammered. 'I'll ask at home.'

'Right then, no problems on that score,' she said with a secretive chuckle. 'You'll earn ten francs for your trouble, but I wouldn't go wasting all that nice money at the fair if I were you.'

When I returned home Aunt asked me how I had got on.

'She asked if I was a virgin,' I replied.

Uncle Werner ducked beneath the counter to hide his laughter, but I was left with a tight feeling in my stomach for the rest of the day.

I was drawn to Miss van Vooren as to the cool blackness of a long-dead star whose gravity is impossible to resist. The light that so unmistakably beamed from her face in the photos of the Catholic Girls' Circle, of which

Aunt too had been a member before she married, had obviously been extinguished at some point in her life.

Shortly after stowing away her useless wedding dress for evermore, she must have resolved to spend the rest of her days casting shade instead, as a sort of antidote to that old sparkle which still made me blink when I stared into her dimness for too long.

As fussily as she specified the meagre purchases which drove every shopkeeper in Stuyvenberghe to despair, so meticulously did she weigh her innumerable invisible ailments on the scales of her words. She was at pains to describe with forensic accuracy the ache in her left hip, which was neither really acute nor dull, and not so much in her muscles as in the bone, although she was certain it wasn't rheumatism . . . maybe it was just that she had a cold, or an infection, it could be a boil, since boils ran in the family.

I asked myself how Uncle Werner could bear to listen to her litanies without feeling terminally ill himself. Miss van Vooren had only to mention her varicose veins, something she was particularly prone to doing when the shop was crowded with customers, for me to feel a blue Nile delta slithering down my own shins towards my heels.

Her lamentations resonated in my limbs, charting every blind spot in my body and shunting me into an endless universe of pain from which I had previously been excluded. Until then I had known only the tropical heatwaves of influenza which, in the dead of winter or early spring, had made me lose myself in deliriously dense rain forests and released me from school.

Wrapped in blankets, I would recline on the sofa in the front room like an oriental deity in the half-light of his sanctuary, roused from his slumber only by the tinkle of the silver spoon in the glass of lemon squash on the tray Aunt brought me several times a day. I would take the glass from her hands like a cup of poison and bravely drink it down in one go, despite the bitterness that made the roots of my hair tingle.

Fever liquefied the days. I fancied I could smell ether or carbolic acid. I fancied I heard wheelchairs rolling squeakily down a hallway long ago, in some castle or other full of nymphs in winged head-dresses and wards with row upon row of dazzling white beds in which the sick lay wrapped in their sheets like caterpillars in silken cocoons.

I heard the whoosh of curtain rails and a voice, possibly Aunt's, calling out: 'Quick, Werner, quick, he's going to be sick again. Hold the basin under his chin.'

Towards evening the wind died. Summer dusk draped itself over the village like a clammy sheet, and at half-past six the church bells set about coaxing the world back into its old routine.

The shop filled up after vespers, which was less than an hour before Aunt's closing time. She called for me to come from the kitchen and lend a hand. Uncle Werner was out, taking his weekly drink at the café.

'The lad's been asked to help carry the canopy,' she remarked while I climbed up the ladder to fetch her a packet of chicory powder from the shelf.

'Really? Isn't he rather young?' said a customer, and someone else remarked on how time flew nowadays.

I handed Aunt the chicory powder and sat on the bottom rung of the ladder, waiting for her next summons.

I had brought the schoolmaster's book, which lay open on my lap. By then I had got to the chapter entitled 'Man Revealed'. Aunt would have hated the pictures.

As early as 1628, read the caption to a diagram of a human heart sprouting antlers of blood vessels, *William Harvey, an English physician, discovered the circulation system in which the blood mass is pumped through the veins by the action of the heart.*

'Quite the little bookworm, that boy,' someone said. 'Nose permanently buried in a book.'

I pretended not to hear.

Not long afterwards, Albrecht von Heller, Swiss biologist and universal genius, described the irritability of muscles and the action of nerve tissue. On the heights of Parnassus, the pioneers of Medicine, Herophilus and Erasistratos, drank a toast of Ambrosia in celebration of the transcendence of the flesh by means of the Electricity of Animation. A great stride forward in the domain of nervous activity!

'He's such a good reader,' said Aunt. 'It's all Greek to me, but he speaks so nice and proper, just like they do on the radio. Go on, Joris, read us something.'

'You won't like it,' I replied, glad of an excuse. 'There, have a look.'

I turned the book around so that everyone in the shop

could see the picture of the atlas vertebra captioned *An appropriate name for the Heroic Bone that supports the Skull.*

'Very complicated, I'm sure,' muttered one of the customers, a farmer's wife who twitched her shoulders and pressed her shopping bag to her stomach every time she opened her mouth.

'Oh, that's what he likes best,' said Aunt. Despite her queasiness she sounded proud. 'But put away that book now, dear, and get me a tin of apricots from up there.'

'Don't want the young folk to get too full of themselves, do we?' she smiled, winking at her clientele.

When I was halfway up the ladder, reaching for the tinned fruit, my attention was caught by two figures on the pavement shielding their eyes against the glare as they peered through the plate glass: a woman who struck me as a bit older than Aunt Laura, and beside her a girl with jet black hair. They both wore wide-brimmed straw hats, and made to step into the shop. I had never seen them before.

The shop bell tinkled. The last customers to have come in twisted round to look, and appeared to recognise the woman. There was a ripple of curiosity and surprise, but the newcomer put her gloved, right-hand forefinger to her lips to silence them. Taking the girl by the hand, and unnoticed by Aunt at the counter, she squeezed past the customers at the back to examine the merchandise in the windows. She ran the tip of her forefinger over the fly swatters, which Uncle had tied in bunches on either side of the displays because there was so much demand for them at this time of year, especially among farmers' wives. The woman apparently found them dusty, for she rubbed her forefinger over her thumb several times.

The girl gave a little neigh of laughter, at which her companion murmured 'Shush'.

They emanated the sort of elegance I had only seen before in photos of my mother's childhood, and in the old fashion magazines on the bottom shelf of the landing cupboard, where Aunt kept a variety of lumber. It was as if there had been a tornado in the night that had scooped up the pair of them, blown them halfway across the country and dropped them in the field just outside the village once the storm subsided.

The woman's gaze wandered over the shelves and the rack of apothecary jars – empty but kept by Uncle for appearance's sake – and stopped at my knees. I was halfway up the ladder holding a tin of apricots.

Then the woman's eyes met mine. Hers were bright blue.

'Monsieur,' she said, inclining her head graciously.

'Monsieur,' echoed the girl, who was standing beside her.

The shop was almost empty when Aunt looked up from her work at last and noticed the newcomers.

'Well I never . . .' she said, coming out from behind the counter to greet them.

'Laure,' said the woman.

'Hélène,' stammered Aunt, untying her apron. 'Quelle surprise!'

She put her apron on the counter and shook hands with the woman, after which they touched their cheeks to each other while pursing their lips.

'Nous sommes arrivées hier soir, pendant l'orage,' said the woman. 'Nous venons de Bruxelles. This young lady has expressed the desire to pay her uncle a visit. Her parents are away in France for a week or two, aren't they, Isabella? Come now, say bonjour to Madame Laure.'

The girl shook hands with Aunt Laura and curtsyed prettily.

'How nice that you have come to pay your dear uncle a visit,' Aunt retorted in a French that sounded a bit halting to my ears, but I felt a stab of envy nevertheless because I could understand only half of what she was saying.

'I think your uncle must feel quite lonely here at times, all alone in the old house,' Aunt went on. 'I'm sure he is very pleased to have visitors.'

The girl seemed unimpressed by the compliment. She spoke French, too. 'He always tells me to be careful and not to tread on the lettuce when I'm playing in the vegetable garden,' she said. 'He says little girls get up to mischief.'

She paused. 'But I'm not a little girl. I'm a young lady, and I have manners.'

'Well well,' Aunt smiled, reverting to Flemish. 'She can stand up for herself all right, that's for sure. A real Van Callant, I do believe. And how is the dear Baron? We haven't seen very much of him lately.'

'He can't wait for the hunting season to begin,' said Hélène. 'It was such a relief for all of us when old Marie agreed to stay on in Monsieur's service after poor Jerome died.'

She turned to me. 'And who is this brave young man on the ladder?'

'Tell Madame your name,' instructed Aunt.

I came down the ladder. 'Joris, Madame. Joris Alderweireldt.'

'Werner's brother's boy,' explained Aunt. 'You remember . . .'

'Oui, je sais . . .' replied Hélène. She turned to the girl, saying: 'The young man's father is deceased. His mother lives in Spain for most of the year.'

'Ah, je comprends,' said the girl, without deigning to look at me.

'Yes indeed,' said Aunt, crossing to the window to let down the blinds. 'Found herself some Juan over there, a bullfighter I shouldn't wonder. Not really in our league, of course . . .'

'Une histoire malheureuse, toute cette affaire,' said Hélène.

Aunt Laura hung the Closed sign on the shop door. 'No doubt about it,' she concurred, 'a very sad business.'

ACCORDING TO MR SNELLAERT, THE VAN CALLANTS WERE of great and glorious lineage, though they had come down in the world of late. It was true that Master Theodore, the last Baron of Stuyvenberghe, did not show his face much nowadays, but we were not to forget that his ancestors had written important chapters of our history with their own blood.

'What does it say on the saints' pedestals in church?' he asked one day during our history lesson. 'What does it say beneath the coat of arms with three golden hinds on an azure ground?'

He waited a while in stern silence to emphasise our ignorance, after which he supplied the answer himself with a wag of his finger: 'Groeninghe Velt! Groeninghe Velt! That's what it says. And what does it mean?'

Despite the fact that the Van Callants spoke better French than Flemish these days, back in 1302, on 11 July to be exact, one of their kin, by the name of Jean, had been a noble warrior thrusting his sword into the bowels of French horses in the mud of the Groeningen Creek and, as the master put it, had made mincemeat of Philip's army between the soup and the spuds.

'Such derring-do, that was,' he continued, as if he had observed the battle from a ringside seat.

'Picture this. All those horses keeling over, kicking like mad, while the lords riding them in heavy armour were deadweights, they just sank. But our Jean didn't stop there. No indeed! Less than two years later, during the battle of Pevelenberg, he fought his way right up to the French king's tent. They say he even drank wine from the king's goblet. Talk about being brave . . .'

In later centuries the Van Callants gradually withdrew to the seclusion of their ancestral home. I myself had seen Master Theodore, Jean's distant descendant, only once in the flesh, and only from afar, sitting doll-like in a wicker chair with a rug over his knees on the front porch of his manor. It was early autumn. My curiosity had got the better of me, so I ignored the PROPRIETÉ PRIVÉ sign at the entrance to the tree-lined alleyway at the back.

It was a becalmed, sun-drenched afternoon, turning chilly towards the end. An orange awning had been extended over the terrace. I heard the sound of a radio, a man's voice speaking a jerky sort of French, followed by piano music.

The breeze battened down the grass on the rise between the pond and the house, and pried the first autumn leaves off the ancient beeches on either side. Looking between the trunks of the trees I could make out the wall of the orchard and overhanging branches laden with ripe pears, then on the other side, protruding above an equally weathered wall, the tips of willow stakes drooping with runner beans.

Half submerged in the stream along the perimeter of the estate there still remained vestiges of the ancient fortress: blocks of yellow stone, bluestone doorsteps, chunks of foundations of the edifice which, as our master would have it, had once dominated the landscape for miles around. One of Master Theodore's ancestors pulled it down and built himself a less grim-looking residence on the same site. Later still another Van Callant dug the pond, thereby modifying the course of the stream, after which the spoil was turned into mounds topped with artfully designed ruins.

Since then the parkland had been left to go to seed, the undergrowth taking over, the pond choked with reeds and silted up by the stream emerging from the backwoods, where there was a statue of a hunting goddess with a beard of moss. The big house itself, the mossy slates on the roof, the flaking blinds over the top-floor windows, the thickly ivied west wing, seemed equally resigned to nature's might. And yet, according to Mr Snellaert, one could not but admire what he called a chapter of living history.

Uncle Werner was less appreciative. 'Sitting on their backsides lining their pockets and checking the state of their stocks and shares, that's all those fat cats ever did,' he would say. 'Haven't hefted a sword in a hundred years.'

Aunt would always protest. Hélène Vuylsteke, for that

was her friend's full name, had been in service at the manor all her life, and the two of them went back a very long way. Aunt always prided herself on the years she had spent with the Sisters of Saint Esprit, at a Walloon boarding-school for girls from good families where it was forbidden to speak a word of Flemish. A posh school, she insisted. She was eternally grateful to Mr Vuylsteke for not only persuading her father to let her accompany his daughter Hélène but also offering to pay more than half of her school fees.

She and her friend pose for the camera in the convent courtyard, either side of a towering nun in a black habit and a close-fitting head-dress like a periscope framing the bulge of her face. In the background roses straggle up the arches of a pergola and a stone heron stoops over water lilies in a pond.

Aunt almost looks as if she wants to hide behind the nun's habit, but Hélène confronts the camera with lifted chin. I recognise the arctic clarity of her gaze, in which a hint of condescension is already to be seen, even though she is barely out of her teens.

'We are not in a hurry,' she had replied that day, when asked whether she would like some coffee, whereupon Aunt had escorted her unexpected visitors to the back.

They would have noticed the flies circling round the ceiling lamp, the oilcloth on the table that gave off a faintly rubbery smell in hot weather, the dresser stacked with cheap crockery and propped-up postcards, and the statue of the Virgin under a dusty bell jar on the mantelpiece between two brass shell cases that served as vases.

I heard Aunt clattering about with the kettle, spoons, sugar tongs, saucers. Perhaps she felt ill at ease with the two pairs of eyes, one steel blue, the other auburn, following her every movement with idle curiosity and amusement.

'I'm still quite happy where I am, living here at Stuyvenberghe,' I heard her call from the scullery where the kettle had just begun to sing, and it sounded almost like an apology.

Hélène Vuylsteke retorted that life was still simple in these parts, and that people in the countryside still knew their place, thank goodness. I don't know if she was being sarcastic.

'I was just thinking of retiring,' she said, 'going to live in my Brussels apartment near the Elsene lakes, but when la petite Isabeau arrived Monsieur Wauthier asked me to take charge of his daughter. He had such good memories of his old bonne . . .' she lowered her voice. 'Between you and me, I am beginning to feel my age rather. Quite a handful, that child.'

'Yes,' said Aunt, coming in with the coffee. 'Runs in the family, doesn't it?'

Hélène nodded. 'Quite the image of her grandmère. A real little chip off the old block.'

The girl was not listening. She had set her hat on the corner of the table and unbuttoned her light raincoat, and her gaze was now sliding over every object in the room with the same aloofness she had shown Aunt and me.

Only when Hélène spoke did she prick up her ears, apparently surprised to hear her governess lapsing into Flemish.

'I can't remember when I was here last,' said Hélène.

'It's been twelve years at least,' Aunt replied. 'Maybe longer.'

The conversation was stilted. I noticed Aunt clenching and unclenching her fingers around her teaspoon.

'I've heard the news about the churchyard,' said Hélène. 'A shame. But the chapel won't have to go, it seems. Monsieur was so pleased.'

In the churchyard the Van Callants had their own abode, a vault against the north transept. All their names were there, chiselled in white marble on either side of a life-size *pièta*, all the knights, ladies, barons and gentlefolk they had ever sired. At some time a plaster scroll had been added at the base of the weeping Virgin, inscribed with the words 'And all Other Members of our Family, scattered across the Face of the Earth, awaiting the Resurrection.'

The lacy carvings on the stone lintels and hefty wrought-iron chains enclosing the steps made their final resting place the most ostentatious structure of all, while the cemetery itself, with its pinnacled tombs of granite on which no expense had been spared, its separate corner for cot deaths and the outlying ranges of sagging headstones in reinforced cement, seemed as status conscious as the village of the living, itself reflected in the churchyard like a willow in a pond.

'Monsieur was not very keen to move his beloved

mother and all his family to a new concession,' observed Hélène. 'Their rightful place, he says, is in the lee of the church.'

'Yes indeed,' said Aunt, 'though we won't be so lucky, will we?'

Hélène ignored the hint of resentment in Aunt's reply. 'It's because they rest in lead coffins, I believe,' she said. 'It seems they can't take anything in or out, not out of lead.'

'Still, it's a bit odd,' said Aunt. 'You'd have thought a person had the right to rest in peace until . . .' she paused, raising her cup to her lips, 'until there's practically nothing left.'

I wondered how much was left of my father. In my imagination the earth under my feet was no more than a thin skin, barely thicker than the ice on the ground during a severe winter. The dead were beneath, drifting like fish in a netherworld of sandy soil and debris, leading an existence devoid of oxygen or hunger. My father was there too, lying on his back with his hands behind his head while he counted the strokes of the church bell, which must have sounded to him like music that had ceased to hold any interest. Perhaps he peered through the chinks between the slabs of the Van Callant vault with the same curiosity that filled me when I peered through the bars of the gate to their ancestral home.

Mr Snellaert, who never missed an opportunity to speechify, assured us that when someone departed this earth he was subsumed into Eternity. The Incandescent Glory of God, he called it. A light so harsh that the wicked would all cover their faces with their hands because they couldn't stand the glare. Only the righteous would approach the Almighty with an open, steady gaze, and they were pretty thin on the ground.

'I can think of some among our number who'll be needing very dark glasses indeed,' he had concluded, without looking at anyone in particular, although we all felt accused.

'Another drop?' offered Aunt Laura, bending over the table with the coffeepot in her hand. 'Such a shame to let it go cold.'

Hélène nodded. The girl was growing restless, pushing her cup away and jiggling her knees.

'Je me sens un peu fatiguée,' I heard her say. 'Can I go out into the garden?'

Hélène glanced at Aunt Laura.

'Mais bien sûr,' said Aunt in a honeyed tone. 'But p'raps the young lady fancies taking a look around the shop. If she's careful not to break anything, I mean.'

I could sense that Hélène Vuylsteke did not appreciate the afterthought.

'Que pensez-vous, Isabeau?' she asked. 'The garden or the shop?'

The girl stood up. She folded the raincoat she had kept on her lap all this time, laid it on the seat of her chair and went out into the passage.

'You run along and keep an eye on her, Joris,' said Aunt.

I stalled for a bit, although I could tell by the nervous tic in her eyelid that she was eager to have a word with Hélène in private.

'Joris!' she repeated, with urgency in her voice.

I moved towards the door exasperatingly slowly.

'What a slowcoach,' I heard Hélène say as I stepped into the passage.

A sigh escaped from Aunt, which I did not know how to interpret. Her fingers drummed on the tabletop.

'I've no idea what he's thinking half the time,' she said. 'Sometimes it's as if the lad lives in a glass box.'

'What about his mother?' Hélène asked.

'I sent her a letter about the headstone. Her brother phoned . . .' Their voices dropped.

I didn't like it when people talked about me behind my back, and it was even worse when they spoke French, which I could more or less follow thanks to Mr Snellaert's lessons but which made my mouth feel as dry as soft sand. It was worse than ever that afternoon, because as I reluctantly moved down the passage I could hear a high-pitched singsong coming from the shop.

Once my eyes became accustomed to the half-light I saw the girl prancing about in the middle of the shop.

'Dolly, jamais je t'oublierai,' she carolled, 'Dolly, toujours je t'aimerai.' She had taken a hairbrush from one of the baskets by the door and was holding it upright in front of her mouth.

She waved her free hand up and down in time to the melody, but now and then, when she lost track of

65

the words and hummed uncertainly, it just hung in the air.

She stopped still in mid-performance, made a little bow towards the shop door and spun round. She was looking in my direction, but I wasn't sure she could see me. Perhaps she just saw my silhouette.

She turned about to face the door again.

'And now for one of my favourite chansons,' she announced. 'Quand le téléphone sonne sonne sonne.'

She seemed neither startled nor in the least embarrassed when I emerged from the gloom of the passage. I don't know how old she was. Not much older than me, at any rate, perhaps even slightly younger. Girls older than me, I believed, had given up dreaming of stardom long ago, so I found it very odd to see someone like her, who had history running in her veins and the clink of chain mail following her around, pretending to be a pop star.

Perhaps she was still too young to sit at her mother's dressing table and smear a still foreign femininity on her cheeks, the way the older girls at the convent school suddenly stopped wearing their hair in plaits and started giggling uncontrollably, as though the first stage of growing up was like being tickled.

They always made me feel as if my knees were abnormally big when I strode past the gate, where they would hang around in clusters, sticking out their tongues or taunting me for having freckles and smelling bad.

I felt a pat on my shoulder and air wafting against my cheek as the girl flounced past.

'We saw the circus arrive,' she said, trailing her fingers along the edges of the shelves behind the counter.

'There was an awfully loud noise, and I was scared . . . It was a lion roaring.' I could hear her skirt brushing against the large bins of un-roasted coffee.

She came out from behind the counter and surveyed the goods in one of the windows. Aunt thought she had a high forehead, and that it was typical. I thought it was because her hair was pulled flat over her scalp and tied at the back. Hélène Vuylsteke struck me as the sort of governess who would use a hairbrush to punish misbehaviour, but Aunt said people of high birth always had high foreheads. She didn't know why, it was just one of those things.

'Too much inbreeding, if you ask me,' Uncle Werner used to say. 'Happens with rabbits, too. Not the foreheads, of course – the ears.'

The girl sat on the bottom step of the ladder and reached for the book Mr Snellaert had lent me. She began to turn the pages without much enthusiasm. Now and then I heard her emit a little sigh of boredom, which sounded to me like a personal summons to relieve the monotony of the moment.

In the commotion following their arrival in the shop Aunt had forgotten to lock the glass showcase in which she kept the most expensive items. One of the little doors was ajar. I snatched a few glistening fruits from a jar of sugared cherries and held them out to the girl, in the space between her nose and the book.

She shook her head and pushed my hand away, but I found it hard to believe she was in the least interested in the page she was looking at, which had no pictures on it.

I had another try with a few bright green pellets from a tall canister. Uncle always sang their praises as a sure remedy for a sore throat or dry cough, and when I put three of them in my mouth at the same time to show him how much I believed him I was blown straight to Alaska on a polar wind of peppermint and eucalyptus. This offer, too, was waved away without so much as a glance at me.

As a last resort I turned to the bottles on the top shelf, where Aunt kept her most treasured wares, her essential oils or whatever they were, which she decanted into glass phials with an eye-dropper and sold to customers wishing to give their preserves an extra zest, or to heighten the taste of cakes baked for special occasions and family visits.

'*Alcohol of orange citrus*' read one of the labels in Aunt's spidery hand, and I always wondered how that colourless liquid could possibly smell so strongly of oranges.

According to Uncle Werner it was all quite straightforward. 'They just put an orange to bed with some alcohol for the night,' he grinned, 'and in the morning the alcohol smells of oranges. That's how I got hitched to your aunt.' It was one of those remarks that sent the blood rushing to Aunt's cheeks.

I picked a small, bulbous bottle from the front row, and carried it in both hands to the girl. Before holding it under her nose I twisted the stopper off. There was an exquisite little squeak in the neck of the bottle, from which a wonderful fragrance immediately floated up.

'Oooh, l'essence d'amandes,' she cooed. She threw back her head and shut her eyes, luxuriating in the smell of almonds.

Encouraged by my success I returned to the glass cabinet in search of other fragrances. I heard the girl doing pirouettes behind my back, and making little scraping noises with her shoes on the floor.

'L'essence, l'essence,' she chanted softly.

Vanilla was bound to be a smell she would approve of. Besides, it was easy to locate, because this substance was treacly and dark instead of clear like the others.

Hardly had I unscrewed the top and turned round when a slap to my cheek sent me reeling against the showcase, more from shock than pain. The bottles rocked on the shelves, a few fell over. Something trickled down my neck. There was vanilla on my fingers. My ears burned.

The girl skirted the counter and ran into the passage, upsetting a couple of soup cans in passing.

'Il m'a frappé,' I heard her wail. 'He hit me, he hit me . . .'

'Dammit, Joris! What are you up to?' called Aunt. I heard them push back their chairs and come into the passage. I took out my handkerchief and tried frantically to mop up the spill, without success.

'He tried to kiss me, the clot,' cried the girl as she

returned with the two women in tow, and before I knew it Aunt had given me a box on the ears.

'Du calme!' cried Hélène Vuylsteke. 'Dratted child, it's not the first time this has happened.'

She grabbed the girl by the hand and gave her arm a sharp tug. 'I think you've been up to your old tricks again, haven't you? Off you go and get your coat.'

The girl trotted to the back.

'Still, no excuse for him to go rummaging in my things,' Aunt hissed in my direction. 'He knows perfectly well to keep his hands off the merchandise.'

She moved to the front door and held it open. The girl squeezed past her and Hélène Vuylsteke, and paused on the threshold to put on her hat.

Hélène shook Aunt Laura's hand: 'Lundi prochain?'

'Right, next Monday,' said Aunt. 'See you then. Au revoir.'

'Au revoir,' said Hélène, with a slight curl of the lip, 'and au revoir to the young gentleman, too.'

Aunt shut the door. 'Some gentleman,' was all she said as she made her way to the back of the house.

When I followed some time later, she was at the table. She had poured herself the remainder of the coffee and now sat with her hands clasping the cup as she stared out of the window, oblivious to the cement slabs of the boundary wall and the Virginia creeper to the side.

Upstairs, I scrubbed my hands to get rid of the vanilla smell. I could hear Aunt clearing the table, making much more noise than usual.

I hoped and prayed that Uncle would not come home just yet, and that he would not be too woozy from his drinks, but less than two minutes later I recognised his whistle and his swaggering tread on the garden path.

Next he would put his hands on her hips as she stood by the sink, and try to kiss her neck.

I dried my hands, went to my room and lay down on my bed while the echoes of their rambling exchange reverberated from the garden wall. I could only make out half of what they were saying, but I knew it was about the vault. My mother's name was mentioned, and goodness knows what else Aunt had to carp about. When she was angry she would wrench open her store of aggravation and tip it out over my or my uncle's head.

After a time the storm abated. Uncle tapped on the door of my room. He sat down on the edge of my bed and put his hand on my knee.

'You mustn't mind too much about your aunt,' he said. 'She's going through the change.' I didn't know what he was talking about.

During supper the only sounds were our spoons scraping the bottom of our plates. Aunt had prepared warm buttermilk with apple slices to which she had added far too little sugar, a sure sign that she was in one of her moods.

I knew that Uncle's slurping irritated her. I could tell by the way one of her eyebrows was raised slightly higher than the other.

'He's dead, Joris,' she said abruptly. 'He's dead. It's terribly sad of course, but so it goes. People die every day.'

She lifted her spoon to her mouth and sipped. 'It's us keeping you. You shouldn't forget that.'

'I won't, Aunt Laura,' I replied meekly, but the whole time I was jamming my toecap against the table leg to feel how much it hurt.

I CHERISHED THE NIGHTS IN THOSE OVERLY LUMINOUS weeks of June. For me the darkness held so much more than merely the absence of illumination. In the early days of that summer, the very last, the unforgiving light could be unspeakably crass.

Thinking back to those June days, I see the cracks between the flagstones in the back yard and long columns of ants lugging grass seeds, dead flies, caterpillars and grains of sand on their shoulders, black ants like Negro slaves, red ones like Arabs dwarfed by minarets of country lilies or beanstalks, and the oriental business of caravanserais, there, against the south wall beneath the drainpipe, but far too hurried and too tiny to grasp in the delicious indolence of those endless afternoons.

Night-time was a repository of everything that had ever existed. Sundown set the solid objects of daytime throbbing and seething in slow motion. Molecule by molecule they shed their contours and unfurled. The night was a vast ocean filled with all the movements ever made by arms, mouths, heads and legs, a primeval soup of gestures gently lapping my body and making my head swim.

I had stopped believing in ghosts by then. Death was among us, a megalomaniac collector who kept his treasures in cigar boxes buried in the earth. There was no swapping, ever. As God's faithful warehouse steward, he dispatched his six-legged minions to pillage all that lay motionless and haul it underground, where he would spread out his booty on the tabletop to study each item with a magnifying glass for the purpose of classification, in readiness for Judgment Day.

Whenever God was minded to create a new person He took a stroll through the caverns of death and cast an amused eye over the fruits of His steward's acquisitive obsession. He slid the graves open as if they were drawers, holding His measuring tape to a leg here, noting the dimensions of a chest or shoulder-blade there. Cupboard-fuls of lips were at His disposal, tiers of double chins. On the walls eyebrows and moustaches were displayed like butterflies mounted in frames; elsewhere nipples and warts were stored in sweet jars.

He was at liberty to pick and choose, was God. Nor was He a stingy type by any means, as Uncle Werner was wont to say, because the old goat had been far from sparing with the titty-meat when He fashioned Aunt's elder sisters.

I was keen to believe him, but there was a niggling feeling of doubt at the back of my mind. Mr Snellaert, too, had once told us about people getting children from a shop, but also that they had to place an order for them with Our Lord first. And say a prayer or two, he had added, half under his breath. He wouldn't tell us where the shop was, not just yet – we'd have to wait until we were a bit older and had a bit more money in our savings accounts.

'We never bought any babbies,' said Uncle when I pressed him to tell me more. 'Your aunt and me, we got one free, gratis, for nothing. That was you.'

He removed the stopper from the decanter of port wine, because it was Sunday, and poured himself a generous drink. Then he took a smaller glass and poured a dram for me – after all, I had taken my First Communion and was no longer in short trousers, so to speak.

Aunt came in from the kitchen. 'Oh, Werner,' she wailed, 'do you really think that's the first thing you should teach him?' Shaking her head, she took the soup plates from the dresser and set them on the table.

Uncle Werner gave me a knowing wink, and when Aunt returned to the kitchen he topped up my glass. 'A feller has to learn to drink, so he can have a few on Sunday . . .'

Having a few drinks meant that the world spun around and you felt like a lord. The port had a cloying sweetness that stuck to the roof of my mouth and left a warm trail through my gullet down to my stomach.

'Mind you, we did do the odd bit of shopping in our time,' Uncle grinned. 'Still do, now and then. But we never have enough money. The babbies lie there in the shop in their wicker baskets, wearing pink and blue caps. But you're not allowed to choose. It's take it or leave it.'

'He's having you on,' Aunt called from the sink. She tipped the potatoes into the colander, the steam from the kitchen curling along the rafters into the room. 'If it was that simple . . .'

I knew he was having me on. In the book Mr Snellaert had lent me there were pictures that appeared to be at odds with his talk of shops where you could buy children, including one of a woman with long wavy hair sitting on the base of a column with her lower body splayed open as if her skin had a zipper in it. Wearing a curiously serene expression, she invited the viewer to admire her innards.

According to the book's author, primitive man already showed a certain awareness of the genital mechanisms. Note, he instructed, the disproportionate size of the ovaries relative to the uterus.

Despite being pretty much in the dark about ovaries, I knew Aunt would recoil in horror if I read her the bits about genital mechanisms. A few days earlier, when she was sitting by the window darning socks, I had stared at her so sceptically, with follicles on my mind, that she had asked if there was something the matter with her nose.

'Another drop, lad?' Uncle Werner whispered. 'One for the road?'

I didn't dare say yes out loud, for fear of alarming Aunt. He poured a splash of the ruby liquid into my glass and gave himself a generous refill. The port was evidently agreeing with him.

'Did they get me from that shop too?' I asked. Through the wooziness in my head I tried to look at him sharply, to show that I knew he was having a laugh.

'Course they did.' He nodded towards the kitchen, and winked at me again. He was generous with his winks after downing a few glasses. 'The first time your mother let me hold you in my arms, the price-tag was still dangling from your elbow . . .'.

He paused. I suspected another joke was in the air.

'You were a free gift, dammit!'

I tried to roar with laughter along with him, although I didn't think much of his wit.

'Werner, please,' hissed Aunt. 'You're doing the boy's head in with your nonsense.'

She set the soup tureen on the corner of the table, put the ladle in and stirred. Uncle Werner patted his paunch contentedly.

'God created the day, and mother created the soup.' He held out his hands to receive his plate.

'Buying children in a shop . . .' snorted Aunt. When she had served us both she sat down and crossed herself.

'You know that children grow inside their mothers. You saw those pictures of your own ma when she was expecting you?'

'But Laura,' Uncle Werner laughed. 'We were just kidding. The boy's no fool . . .'

I saw her casting baleful looks at the glass of port beside my plate.

'That shop . . .' she said, lifting her spoon to her lips and blowing on it before taking a sip, '. . . they never let me in . . . not that I didn't stand on the doorstep waiting and waiting . . . Always closed.'

An awkward silence fell.

Looking up from my plate I noticed that Aunt was scowling at Uncle Werner from under her furrowed brow, and that her eyes were rimmed with pink.

Uncle sank his spoon in his soup and chewed his lower lip.

'Go on, Joris, eat,' said Aunt coolly.

After lunch I caught the sound of her muffled squeals and strangely sinuous giggles drifting down the stairs. She and Uncle Werner had gone up for a rest, to settle their stomachs, as Uncle put it.

I wondered why Aunt gave all those little yelps and why there was such a lot of creaking, as if they were chasing each other across the floorboards in the attic. Perhaps Uncle was gripping her firmly by the waist and lifting her up to give her a good shake, although it was also possible that he was lying on top of her, as I had spied him do through a chink in their bedroom door one day, and that he was rubbing his stomach over hers, presumably to help settle the food. Uncle often said his wife needed a good cuddle from time to time, or she'd go sour.

They had left me alone with the dishes, as usual on such occasions. I rinsed the plates under the tap and put them to drain in the rack over the sink.

Now and then I paused in my labours to take another sip of port. I had been careful not to drain my glass during supper and had smuggled it into the kitchen. I wanted to drink it slowly so as to make the lightness in my head last as long as possible.

I scoured the sink and caught myself grinning stupidly at the metallic sound of the steel pad against the sides, which reminded me of the mewing of a cat.

The day was decked in gold leaf. Aunt's twitters were like a flurry of petticoats up and down the house, invoking the guileless girl she must once have been, as she was in all those snapshots of her childhood: the youngest in a row of nine flaxen-haired children arrayed around their adored, basalt-hewn mother, posing in the yard behind the farmstead where she grew up.

Later, too, sitting on a rug under a silver willow in the field by the canal with half a dozen girlfriends, teenagers like herself, she is admittedly the only one brazen enough to look up from her knitting, but her gaze reflects little more than the tender greening of springtime.

At her back Hélène Vuylsteke and Miss van Vooren recline rather fetchingly against the tree. Miss van Vooren clasps her hands behind her neck, the jacket of her two-piece suit unfastened to admit the sunshine, but her blouse is primly buttoned all the way up to her chin.

Our excursion took us Over the Hills and Far Away was the somewhat hyperbolic caption penned by Aunt with white ink in the album, which abounded in pictures of prayer meetings as well as pious evening singsongs around Miss van Vooren's harmonium. She herself called the instrument 'my house organ', which seemed an absurd name for the ramshackle, wheezy apparatus that sent those offensive, nasal tones floating over the cobbles on Saturdays.

The harmonium would always be open when I came to deliver Miss van Vooren's groceries, the musical score of some hymn on the stand, presumably to impress her extraordinary piety on anyone who happened to call, but several of the ivories had been chipped or lost over the years, so the keyboard resembled an old man's gap-toothed grin.

Aunt Laura had fond memories of the scenes in her album. Each outing must have been like going halfway across the world, for she had rarely travelled further than Bruges or Ghent. She had been to the seaside once or twice, to Ostend, which she remembered well because she and Uncle Werner had spent their honeymoon there, in a small hotel where they served inexpensive meals, as she told me excitedly on the day she bought two return tickets to the seaside as a treat for my First Communion. As it turned out we lost our way as soon as we got there – the small hotel had long since been demolished.

She did go abroad once, to Lourdes, on a train crammed with crutches and cripples with miraculous expectations, and they had a short stop in Paris, just long enough to pose for a group portrait at the Trocadéro, under the watchful eye of a most combative-looking Hélène who, with Miss van Vooren's help, unfurled the banner of the

Catholic Girls' Circle, thereby hiding most of the Eiffel Tower from view.

Two pages further on in the album she is at home, swamped in a sea of bouquets in the living room on her wedding day. She smiles nervously at Uncle, who makes an equally starched impression, as if his mother had given his suit a quick iron with him already in it.

At the registry office my father signs the marriage certificate as a witness, while Uncle and Aunt look on with a rather dazed expression, but out in the orchard, the formalities over and done with, he stands shoulder to shoulder with his slightly less robust look-alike, twin brothers, cigarettes between their lips, shirt collars undone, tipsy and dreamy, like me that Sunday, lulled by the port wine, setting the roasting pan upside down by the sink and hearing Aunt's little cries tumbling from the eaves like fledgling sparrows.

After a while I heard Uncle's racking cough. I was afraid he would suffocate, but the next moment he was stumping across the landing. He breezed into the kitchen, whistling.

'Good lad,' he said, grunting with the afterglow of a gratification located I knew not where within his body. 'Done all the dishes for us, all on your own.'

He pulled his braces down and held his forearms under the tap.

'Had a good rest?' I asked. 'Did the food settle down all right?'

'Don't you worry,' he said, slapping water on his jowls. 'Pass me the towel, will you.'

He mopped his face. 'Just as well Our Lord created Sundays. When else can a body catch up on his homework?'

'But you always tick me off when I leave my homework till Sunday,' I said.

Squaring his shoulders, he gave me an amused look. 'That's because I'm the boss and you're not. You can't even piss in a straight line yet.'

He flicked the drops clinging to his fingers on to my face.

On the square in front of the station the fairground attractions were covered by tarpaulins in assorted colours, like the tents of Mongolian horsemen. Through the slits glimmered an occasional glass eye, a harness decorated with little mirrors, the tip of a black-painted hoof. The circus tent was pitched in a fallow field on the other side of the track, its roof supported by two masts from which banners hung limply in the afternoon stillness.

The streets were desolate, they smelt of asphalt and heat. I was still a little dizzy from the port, but had a sense of sobering up. The comforting haze that had been stretched taut like a membrane over the world began to tear, letting in trickles of the sadness that engulfed me at times for no reason, even though I was only twelve.

Each year I awaited the arrival of the travelling fair with mixed feelings. The other boys couldn't wait to jump on their bikes after school and descend on the square by the station like a plague of locusts, or stop at the side of the road and marvel at the slow motion of a camel's rumi-nations, whereas I preferred to walk past with studied nonchalance, permitting myself no more than the most fleeting of glances.

The caravans were inhabited by coffee-coloured folk whom the villagers regarded with suspicion for being like jackdaws, pinching everything in sight. Everyone said so, but Aunt had different ideas. They were good customers, she said, and coffee-coloured or not, she had never had any trouble with them at all.

They usually sent their daughters to the shop for their provisions, amber-eyed girls in saris and hair ribbons of a purple so bright it left me speechless.

Not that they said much either, for they would extract from the depths of their shopping bag a scrap of paper covered in hieroglyphs, which for some strange reason Aunt could only decipher by taking her reading glasses from her apron pocket and putting them on her forehead instead of her nose, holding the note at arm's length, then bringing it up close to her eyes and holding it out again, as if the recondite script did not read from left to right but from far to near.

The purple girls eyed her dispassionately all the while. They slipped into every shop with the same quiet demeanour and laid their illegible shopping lists on the counter. They were the harbingers of topsy-turvy times for the village. To me the roundabouts, rides and stalls were magical machines, not entirely to be trusted in their garish glitter. The morning after the trailers all vanished in the night and the station square stood empty once more, a flotsam of late revellers staggered about the pavement, grabbing hold of drainpipes and doorknobs to steady themselves, as though fearful of losing touch with the ground underfoot.

'Well, they certainly look like plucked chickens,' sniffed Miss van Vooren, who refused to venture out of doors after Mass until the final strains of fairground music had died away. For days on end she remained ensconced in her house amid the lofty cedars, keeping the windows blinded against brass bands, dance parties and drunkards.

Once the fair was over the world sank back into the swoon of summer, where time did not count. Mr Snellaert stored away his solar system, collected the inkwells from the desks, pronounced his Last Judgment and shut the book of latitudes with a firm clap.

On very quiet nights, when I went to bed with the window open I could hear, high in the sky above, a faint rumbling sound, a ruffling like feathers being spanned, the tock of spatulas or hammers, the clatter of chains hauling heavy objects, as if up there, in God's own belfry, the Great Miller had secretly opened the roof lights to the breeze blowing around the spire and was now funnelling it away into a range of small basins, catching the remainder in sacks to be stored in the recesses of a vast mill.

In my imagination He was a flour-dusted eccentric who took no more notice of the Gloria during Mass than if it were being sung on the radio, not bothering to raise His eyes from His workbench in the space behind the clock-face, which was where He busied Himself with pliers and tweezers to create new insects, where He lingered among catalogues full of Milky Ways trying to decide which, if any, merited inclusion in the firmament.

The clock had struck half-past three. I headed down the church lane towards the stream, following the footpath along the railway embankment where the hot air shimmered above the rails and conjured an expanse of water on the horizon.

Nothing stirred in the fields. It was only when I reached the tree-lined alleyway that a blackbird or two swooped down from the lindens to catch worms in the ruts cut by cart-wheels.

I began to feel drowsy. Thanks to all the food I'd eaten I gradually became susceptible to gravity again. The port was wearing off.

I stretched out my arms and turned around a few times to get things spinning again, while whorls of dust rose about my ankles. Then I leaned back against a poplar and slithered down. Looking up into the leafy crown, I noticed how the tracery of branches resembled dark veins in the sunlit canopy.

I was half sunken in a slumber perfectly attuned to the soporific afternoon when I thought I heard someone approaching. A moment or two later someone kicked my foot.

I opened my eyes and saw a pair of hands gripping the cane of a furled umbrella, and, further up, a chin, pinched lips, and then large sunglasses.

'Joris,' Miss van Vooren said crossly, 'is this any way for a bearer of the heavens to behave?'

IT BECAME UNBEARABLY HOT IN THE DAYS THAT FOLLOWED. Uncle Werner said you could fry eggs on the cobbles and that the brewer would be rubbing his hands with glee if the weather kept up for the rest of the week.

In the garden behind the village hall the chairs and tables had already been set up around the dance floor. The village girded itself up to be at the epicentre of the world for the next three days. I didn't like it. It muddled up my own circles.

On Friday evening around seven the strains of a brass band could be heard in the shop, the pounding on the bass drum, the blare of slide trombones. Beyond the churchyard, in the high street, children stood watching a parade of girls in white busbies. They were twirling batons.

'Don't you want to go and have a look?' Aunt asked. 'What's stopping you? You're doing precious little just sitting there . . .'

I didn't care one way or the other. Nor did I care that Uncle Werner had bought tickets for the circus, as he had been reminding me all week, pretending it was all for my sake, when he was the one who couldn't wait to get his best suit on.

Around half-past seven Aunt locked up and began to apply her make-up. She was still put out about the incident in the shop, and any mention of it was enough for her to throw me a look of icy contempt. There were certain places in the house that, as far as she was concerned, were sacred. Any trespass amounted to dishonouring Aunt in person, and she did not forgive lightly. One of those places was the glass showcase in which she kept the essential oils. Uncle himself had evidently learned his lesson, because he always summoned her from the kitchen when a customer asked for lavender oil.

Equally out of bounds was her dressing table, which stood in a corner of their bedroom. A splay-legged piece of furniture, glass-topped, with several drawers and a triple mirror, it was a shrine to the girlish vanity she had long since abandoned, though she sometimes caught a stale whiff of its aroma as she sat on her salmon pink, muslin-frilled stool, with her hands flat on the glass before her, studying her three-way reflection.

I never saw her brush her hair at her dressing table. She always did that down in the kitchen, in front of a small lozenge-shaped mirror that hung by the door to the stairs, even though she had to go through all sorts of contortions to get a full view of her face while she stuck hairpins behind her ears or suddenly pursed her lips in an expression of unwonted coquetry, as though poised to give her reflection a smacking kiss.

She used a lot of blue eye shadow that was far too bright for her, as was the shade of her lipstick; she applied lashings of mascara which after a couple of hours would leave a curve of spidery black flecks on her cheekbones. I thought she looked rather silly, but Uncle loved to see her all dolled up.

He called her 'my girly'. Sometimes he would creep up behind her when she was busy and give her a smack on her bottom with the flat of his hand. She would fend him off with a thrust of the hips and, much to my amazement, throw back her head so he could nuzzle her throat.

'Women. Just you watch out,' was his customary response when he saw the surprise on my face.

Somewhere in the book lent to me by the master it said that the psychologies of male and female were distinct, women being more inclined to domesticity, caring and tenderness than men, who still had the hunting instinct coursing through their veins.

Uncle Werner, though, struck me as more of a harmless shaggy dog in a basket by the stove, a cascade of droopy ears and vertical folds, from whose depths an eye blinked lazily from time to time, or a great yawn escaped. Having polished his shoes to a high sheen, he began to tie his laces, whistling a jaunty tune.

'Time to be off now,' Aunt announced, screwing the lid back on the small jar of rouge. And with a bright blue wink in my direction: 'We don't want to spoil your fun now, do we?'

*

We made our way across the churchyard to the high street, where we joined the throng heading to the square by the train station. There had been a sudden shift of focus within the village, which left the church looming desolately in the waning day, notwithstanding the weathercock on the spire being set ablaze by a last ray of sunshine.

Behind the village hall the women danced in pairs over the boards. Under one of the chestnut trees, a young man with a plastered quiff and glitzy suit stood on a podium singing 'Seven Carnations, Seven Roses', accompanied by drums and bass guitar. The trees were festooned with coloured lights, and crowding around the beer stand were farmers, thumbs hooked in their waistcoats, exchanging tall stories.

The rides and roundabouts were still covered with tarpaulins, but in the field on the other side of the railway track the top of the circus tent was brilliantly lit. The purple girls were checking tickets at the entrance. They were wrapped in glittery scarves, and the dusk made the pools of their eyes deeper than ever. Their irises sparkled glass-like in their coppery faces. When I showed my ticket I felt as if they were looking straight through me, counting my ribs.

'How are you doing, girls?' Aunt crowed, all mercantile heartiness. She poked me in the back for me to greet them as warmly as she did.

Uncle Werner had already disappeared into the tent to find us good seats. He was waiting by the front row, close to the ring, and motioned us to hurry up.

'At least he's given up on the trains,' Aunt sighed, in response to someone's remark about boys and their toys.

No sooner had we sat down than Aunt cried, 'Look! Your fiancée's here too.'

She was sitting beside Hélène Vuylsteke in one of the boxes, the most expensive seats facing the orchestra pit and the curtain, upon which a circle of light was projected. She wore a dark blue hat with a large bow and a puff-sleeved dress. I registered a bracelet gleaming on her wrist as she turned to Hélène and pointed at the masts and rigging in the big top, where the trapezes hung.

She must have primped and preened before going out. At the big house she was bound to have her own dressing table, strewn with her mother's powder compacts and tooled-leather jewellery boxes full of sparkly rings and pin-sharp earrings. From the way her shoulders were swaying back and forth I could tell she was swinging her legs.

Hélène Vuylsteke gave Aunt Laura a nod of greeting, and Aunt nodded back. When I followed suit it took a while for my nod to be acknowledged – a bit sourly, I fancied.

The girl sat watching the people taking their seats and did not appear to have noticed me. For the past few days the slap she had given me had kept coming back like a boomerang to strike my neck. The slightest inattention to my sums in class was enough to send me crashing against the showcase all over again, with the imprint of her hand branded on my cheek.

Aunt was convinced it was all my fault, but Uncle had

smiled and said: 'Well, my boy, once you fall into a woman's clutches, that's it.'

Women. Their words were always so much more charged than men's. They dabbed colours on their cheeks and sprayed their underarms with lily-of-the-valley scent. At the hairdresser's they were amazons riding chrome chairs with steel helmets on their heads, eyes squeezed shut like cats dozing on the windowsill until such time as the steam began to rise from their curls. And they were known to sprinkle strange substances into food – like witches.

'Bromide in the soup!' I heard Aunt exclaim over the hubbub in the shop one day. 'Keeping the flags down then, are you?'

The laughter on the other side of the counter made me cringe.

The lights in the tent went down, the buzz of voices died away. The band sounded off a drum roll followed by a fanfare of trumpets, and stepping out from behind the curtain were the purple girls in shiny leotards with purple beads round their ankles. They did a pirouette, fluttering their arms gracefully over their heads as the curtain divided to reveal a man in jodhpurs and riding boots and a white carnation on his tailcoat lapel. He strode to the centre of the ring, spread out his arms and boomed: 'Mesdames Messieurs, bonsoir! Good evening to you all!'

He crossed to the other side of the ring, where the girl

and Hélène were sitting in their box, made a gallant bow and boomed with mock deference: 'Your highness . . .'

There was a ripple of laughter from the benches. The girl glanced up at Hélène Vuylsteke, unsure of how to behave.

'Oh my, such a fine-looking feller,' Aunt sighed, and she started clapping along with everyone else. 'Dark Eyetalian type . . .'

'Fake tan,' Uncle grumbled. 'Laid it on with a trowel, he has.'

The Italian returned to the middle of the ring. A marvellous time would be had by all, he promised, 'an evening of death-defying, daring and dangerous feats of fantasy, graciously accompanied by Freddy Brack und seine Capelle with Viva España, and for your special delectation, ladies and gentlemen, our first spectacle, all the way from France – Mario Marconi and his calibrated zebras!'

The trumpets sounded and the purple girls clacked their castanets.

'Oh good show!' Uncle enthused. 'My favourite – dobbins in pyjamas!'

I saw Aunt nudging his thigh with the back of her hand a few times, but he took no notice.

The zebras wore yellow plumes on their heads and cantered round the ring, driven by a trainer with a whip. His naked torso was bound with leather straps so tight his flesh bulged out on all sides.

The whip cracked, the zebras trotted on the spot, turning on their axis. There was a burst of applause. The girl was jigging up and down on her seat with excitement. Hélène Vuylsteke shushed her, lifted the hat with the big bow from her head and smoothed her hair.

The act ended with all the zebras rearing up in close formation. Hardly had the tail of the last one vanished behind the curtain when the clowns Titi and Toto waddled into the ring in their oversized shoes. They sat on the same invisible chairs as last year and Uncle almost fell off his own out of sheer hilarity.

'Werner, do try to control yourself,' Aunt sighed, but when Titi lowered himself on to a bedpan attached to a string which was jerked away by Toto at the last moment, Uncle almost died laughing.

'What a scream,' he gasped, holding his sides.

Aunt was embarrassed.

Next came a sketch with a bucket of confetti and a stepladder with wonky rungs, and before the women had finished dabbing their eyes with their handkerchiefs the following act was already being announced: Nina Valencia and her ten grass-green poodles.

Then there was an African woman wearing a cape made of live parrots which turned out to speak five languages, after which came Professor Pillule and his fabulous flea circus, then Mariska and Petruschka, the sisters of the flying trapeze, and a conjuror who sawed himself in two before vanishing in a puff of brown smoke. After him came Pasha, the world's second-largest elephant, sagging in the beam like an ancient galleon, with a chimp in a tutu riding on his back.

Pasha juggled a beach ball, sat up and begged, and, for the grand finale, balanced upside down on one foreleg while the ape swung from the elephant's tail, baring its teeth and screeching.

'Capital!' cried Uncle Werner.

Freddy Brack's German-sounding combo regaled the audience with a thumping pot-pourri of Sicilian salsas, during which time four men in boiler suits assembled the cage for Xerxes, Lion of Mesopotamia, Emperor of the Tigris.

The lights dimmed. A single spotlight was trained on the curtain and a drum rolled menacingly, but Xerxes' entry was something of a letdown. He shambled lazily into the ring, hauled himself up on a tabouret and gave a bored yawn as he waited for his trainer, a young fellow in a suit covered in metal studs.

The lion had to jump through a burning hoop and obliged with such disdain that he drew only a feeble round of applause, but when he opened his jaws wide to accommodate his trainer's head, everyone held their breath.

The girl pressed her hands to her mouth with such an aghast look I doubted its sincerity. While the trainer ticked off one to ten on his fingers to the accompaniment of much drum-rolling, the beast held still, eyes cast dolefully upwards at the big top, as if it were at the dentist.

'Ten!' roared the audience. The trainer retracted his head from the lion's maw to a burst of trumpets. The crowd heaved a sigh of relief.

'Capital!' said Uncle Werner. 'Bravo!'

The band launched into a waltz. The cage was dismantled.

'And now,' the Italian announced, 'the time has come for the star of this evening. A clairvoyant consulted by the great and the good all over the world. The genius of the gimlet eyes to whom all souls are bared, the visionary who has successfully foretold numerous earthquakes — fortunately for us they were all in Manchuria. Mesdames et Messieurs, behold the Oracle of Delphi, the Man who knows no pain, the Mysterious Seer Zaromander . . .'

The purple girls writhed like snakes to the thin notes of a flute, the curtains drew apart and into the ring stepped a tall, slim figure wearing a black cloak adorned with stars and a turban flashing with emeralds.

The clairvoyant swung the cloak over his shoulder, folded his arms across his bare chest, and fixed his gimlet eyes on where the girl and Hélène Vuylsteke were sitting.

'Zaromander?' sneered Aunt. 'His name's André van Lerberghe, nothing fancy about that. Came into the shop for two tubes of toothpaste and a packet of razor blades.'

The clairvoyant now swung his cloak sideways over his extended arm, releasing a flurry of rose petals while a small crown tumbled down out of nowhere. The man caught it in mid-air, ran to the edge of the ring and offered it to the girl on bended knee.

Hélène Vuylsteke motioned the girl to lean forward. Zaromander drew himself up and placed the crown on her head. She held out her arm, offering him the back of her hand, which he brushed with his lips respectfully.

'How does he know she's from the big house?' Uncle Werner wondered aloud. 'How can he tell? It's beyond me . . .'

Meanwhile the clairvoyant went over to a woman elsewhere in the audience. This time a shake of his cloak produced a pair of teddy bears. 'For the twins, Madame,' he said solemnly. The circus tent buzzed with astonishment.

'He got Mariette from the café to fill him in on all the gossip for five hundred francs,' said Aunt. 'That chap's as clairvoyant as a blind man with a glass eye . . .'

'You can say what you like,' said Uncle, refusing to let her dampen his spirits, 'it's still extraordinary.'

The clairvoyant concluded his show with a last supper of razor blades strung together, on which he pretended to gag as he retreated a few paces, clutching his bulging cheeks with both hands. A thread hung from his lips. He opened his mouth and amid mounting applause pulled the string of blades from his mouth.

'So now we know what he needed all those razors for,' said Aunt with a sigh.

The Italian emerged from the wings, followed by all the artistes. The purple girls turned somersaults, jets of water spurted from the clowns' eyes, confetti fluttered down and the lights came on.

'Well, that was well worth the effort,' said Uncle. He stood up and adjusted the creases of his trousers.

Hélène Vuylsteke and the girl had gone. When we came

outside I saw the gamekeeper's car pulling away. He must have been waiting in the road for the end of the show so he could drive them straight home afterwards.

In the garden the chap with the quiff crooned a golden oldie: 'In the Forest Roam the Hunters'.

Uncle took her arm, saying: 'What d'you say to a glass of beer, a nibble of your ear, a twirl around the floor and maybe something more? What about it, eh, Laura?'

'Get away with you, silly . . .'

'No, really, I mean it. How long has it been since we had a little dance, you and me?'

She hesitated.

'It's all right, I can get myself home,' I said. 'Got to be up early tomorrow anyhow.'

Several days ago Miss van Vooren had sent the canopy bearers a note, in the flowing but somewhat sterile hand so familiar to me from her shopping lists, telling everyone, in particular the new member, to be sure to present themselves at the sacristy at least half an hour ahead of time.

'Come on, Laura, be a sport,' Uncle Werner pleaded.

Finally she shrugged her shoulders and said: 'Oh all right then, why not.'

They gave me the key to the front door.

The graves in the churchyard were still giving off heat. The hot air remained trapped between the headstones, and in the deep shadows beneath the linden trees I thought I heard a noise. It sounded like leaves rustling in the wind, which was odd as there had not been a breath of wind for days.

I did not dare look sideways. I heard a match being struck.

'Hey mate,' a man's voice spoke behind me. 'Still up at this hour? You'd better get yourself to bed pronto.' Someone tittered.

I quickened my step until I reached the road on the other side. I had heard Aunt complaining to Miss van Vooren about un-Catholic shenanigans in the church-yard.

'You know what I mean . . .' she had added with a nod in my direction, which I took to signify she was speaking of things for which my ears were yet too tender.

I slipped the key into the lock and let myself in. In the kitchen I filled a glass of water and drank it down. Outside, an electric guitar twanged 'Roses for Sandra' over the rooftops.

My bedroom was as hot as an oven. I got undressed and lay down on top of the bedclothes.

I heard footsteps out in the road, followed by the crunch of gravel. I heard someone moan 'Ronnie, ooh Ronnie.' I stood up and crossed to the window. Under one of the lindens I glimpsed something moving, hands fumbling under a checked skirt, a flash of bare thigh.

I brought my face up close to the window screen to get a better view, and immediately heard a gruff voice, the same one as before, calling out: 'Back to bed with you, I said. Sleep tight, mind the bugs . . .'

I jumped into bed and switched off the bedside lamp. After a while I heard footsteps again, dying away over the cobbles, and around two in the morning I woke with a start to hear Uncle blundering up the stairs.

'Seven carnations, seven roses, for you my sweet these posies . . .' he slurred.

'Shush, Werner,' hissed Aunt.

'. . . Roses and posies . . . for you.'

He bumped into something. Aunt gave a shriek. I wanted to leap out of bed to help, but then I heard her giggle, no doubt because he had seized her by the hips again.

The door of their room clicked shut behind them.

For as long as it took me to fall asleep I heard her intermittent squeals bouncing off the churchyard wall.

I HAVE ONLY ONE PHOTO OF THAT SUNDAY. UNCLE MAY WELL have taken several, since he was hardly likely to have fetched out his camera from the cabinet purely because I had turned up for breakfast in the dazzling white shirt that Aunt had ironed so carefully. He must have had it all planned, and Aunt Laura was probably in on it too. He seldom took photographs, and never on a whim. Perhaps the rest of the pictures were distributed among other albums, gone to family relations, forgotten over time.

I remember Aunt making me wear knee socks, too, although you can't see them here. I am way down in the bottom right-hand corner, you can see one of my arms resting on the table, and although Uncle photographed me from behind you can tell I am looking at Aunt. She is putting a blouse on over her bodice. It floats ethereally over her shoulders; a second or two later it will be buttoned up.

Behind her the window is a bleak rectangle of whiteness, a white that seems to leach into my shirtsleeves. It casts a wintry pall over the objects in the room, making them appear both paler and darker than they presumably were. Aunt's frame seems to be dissolving at the edges, suggesting auras hovering about her limbs.

I love that photo. For the newspaper on the table, which I am touching with my fingertips, for the disarray of cups and coffeepots and spoons, the unprepossessing luxury of breadcrumbs and used plates, but also for being the last one of its kind.

The light in the room is so bright that the reflection in Aunt's eyes makes her pupils look like minute white saucers. In my memory that morning had a very different texture: warmer and more coppery toned. A feverish Sunday at the end of June, with a breeze fluttering the linden leaves like handkerchiefs.

I was only a few paces short of the sacristy facing on to the churchyard, where the others were already waiting. There were three of them, teenage boys slouching against the wall of the church and of an age to wear what they liked, how they liked, such as caps and long hair and trendy collarless shirts. The collar of my own shirt was worthy of a sailing ship. I looked like the kind of boy I'd want to avoid if I chanced upon him on a deserted street corner.

I tried to move close enough to the youths to make it look as if I sort of belonged, and yet not so close as to draw attention to myself. The tallest of the trio was telling jokes, at which I heard myself laugh too heartily.

When they started about girls, in particular one called Claudia and what they called her milk-wagons, I sensed in their sniggers an urgency that was not yet mine. It gave me a feeling of superiority, which I thought best to dissemble.

The tallest one said he had done it three times already, but the others shook their heads disparagingly. Gusta Coremans did not count, not really. She went off with anyone who gave her stickers of pop stars.

I saw her in the shop sometimes. She was an only child. She and her mother, who was quite old, lived in an estate cottage sagging on the verge of collapse under the weight of its own roof tiles. She had frizzy hair which defied every hairbrush, and a slight squint.

Miss van Vooren said you could hardly blame the poor lamb for not knowing who her father was, but there was something decidedly odd about the Coremans twosome. When it was busy in the shop someone would always find a cause to mention that Gusta's mother had been in service at the big house once upon a time. This was common knowledge, as was the fact that Gusta was illegitimate.

'Gusta, Gusta,' the other two boys chanted, to wind up the tallest. 'Gusta Coremans!' They held out their arms and staggered about as if they were about to fall.

'That's got nothing to do with it,' growled the tall boy, and I didn't understand what he meant, because Gusta could have been my sweetheart, too.

It was because she had more balcony than the opera, as Uncle Werner remarked one day, that I felt a surge of pity whenever I saw her coming into the shop, half hidden behind her gigantic shopping bag, big enough to take a whole calf.

When she reached the end of her shopping list came the moment I dreaded most of all. Her ma sometimes gave her five francs spending money.

On such occasions I usually called to Aunt in the kitchen for assistance. She was more persuasive than me, but if she was out I had no choice but to sort it myself.

Gusta took ages to make up her mind. Her indecision brought tears to my eyes. I think it was a question of not wanting to decide. She would spend an eternity drooling over the sweet jars, devouring the contents with her eyes, and then start asking about the pictures inside the chocolate wrappers — were they of pop stars? She must have known her measly five francs did not run to chocolate.

Usually I would mumble something about them all being of factories. I preferred to disillusion her than make her feel poor. In the end she was likely to settle for a string of sugar-pearls, which she would hang round her neck and begin to nibble as soon as she got on her bike.

Some said it was written all over her. She was a Van Callant and no mistake. Miss van Vooren thought so, too. At some point the poor kid must have got wind of what was being said behind her back. You could tell by the way she rode her bike: so hunched over that her back was practically parallel to the road surface and her head bent low over the grotesque shopping bag swinging from the handlebar.

*

When the bell finished striking nine there was a rattling sound on the other side of the sacristy door, and the boys stopped talking. The door opened and Miss van Vooren greeted us with 'How nice, the disciples have arrived.' She was trying to sound casual.

She wore her usual outfit for special occasions: navy blue coat and skirt, flat shoes, milky nylon stockings and a blouse with an enormous bow. She had clearly been to the hairdresser: her head looked twice its normal size.

For two days running she had told Aunt she was sorry but she couldn't stop because she had an appointment at the salon, as though the sanctification of her tresses had to be undertaken in stages, or they would not stand erect as a finely meshed helmet of individually lacquered hairs.

Miss van Vooren let us into the sacristy. The priest was leaning against the wardrobe, practising his sermon. He nodded curtly, without taking further notice of us.

In a while he would be pontificating about the church being like a vessel tossed on an ocean of green meadows, a shipload of Christians on the high seas of time, and he would cite the apostles during the storm at the Sea of Galilee.

Not being an inventive preacher, he came out with the same sermon each year, but his dramatic delivery, complete with flailing elbows and shaking knees, was so convincing that half the congregation would be affected by seasickness.

Propped against the wall, between the clock and the

window, was the canopy: a square of white damask brocaded with gold thread, hanging slackly between carrying-poles of dark wood.

'It's not as difficult as it looks,' Miss van Vooren assured me. 'The main thing is to keep in step with the others, and to carry your pole at the same height . . . Right, I'll get the clothes.'

She inspected the three wide drawers in the lower half of the sacristy closet. Lying in the bottom one were the white vestments with lace borders and a bunch of crimson cords that served as belts.

'Arms up,' ordered Miss van Vooren, turning to me. The others were left to put on their albs themselves, which they did with girlish enthusiasm. Miss van Vooren obviously thought I could not manage without her assistance.

'Put your hands together . . .' She had to stand up on tiptoe to pass the canvas sling over my shoulders, for I was already taller than her.

'A wee bit too long for you,' she remarked, eyeing my alb. 'But we can make it shorter, like this.' She tied one of the crimson cords round my waist.

'Rosa . . .' called the priest from the other end of the sacristy. 'Can you spare me a moment? I've got my head stuck in the sleeves again.' He was swaddled in fabric from the waist up.

'Just a second,' she replied, rolling up my sleeves. Then she turned away to help the priest.

It was some time before his head, flushed purple from exertion, emerged from his surplice.

The boys tried to stifle their sniggers.

'Quite the glamour puss in that get-up, aren't you,' said the tall boy, confronting the shortest of the trio. 'I might even fancy you myself . . .'

'Look a bit of all right, do I?' smirked the short boy, wiggling his hips and lifting his lacy hem between thumb and forefinger.

'Confound all these trappings,' grumbled the priest. 'Imagine if Our Lord had been obliged to get all togged up every time he opened his mouth. He'd have stayed in Nazareth, I wager . . . Wouldn't blame him, either. Spot of sawing, bit of joinery — good honest work.'

Out in the chancel the regular altar boys busied themselves with the liturgical vessels. Up in the rood loft the schoolmaster played the opening chords of *As the hart panteth after the water brooks, so panteth my soul after thee, O God.*

'Now boys! Stop that nonsense and go and sit in the stalls, over there,' she said, indicating the far side of the high choir.

'The youngest first,' she called after us, 'and in an orderly fashion, please.'

The church was filling up. Over half the seats were already taken, and still the door in the entrance kept creaking open and shut with new arrivals.

Over by the communion rail were the chairs upholstered in wine-red velour, the preserve of the gentry since time immemorial. I noted Hélène Vuylsteke seating herself on one of them. She removed her hat, crossed herself, and knelt.

She was alone. Perhaps her charge was still asleep in bed. Perhaps the child simply didn't fancy attending Mass. It had been years since a Van Callant occupied a seat in the premier section of this house of worship, where the sunbeams seeping through the stained-glass windows reassembled into the family coat of arms on the flagstones. The noble family had donated confession boxes, processional banners, incense burners and the occasional relic, they had contributed land to the almshouses and riches to the church treasury. Even the wainscoting at my back was carved with their old battle-cry 'Groeninghe Velt! Groeninghe Velt!'

Above my head Saint Paul leaned heavily on his sword. On top of the choir stalls across the way stood Saint Peter, displaying the keys of heaven to the congregation while a ribbon of incense curled up round his feet. Two of the regular boys were blowing on the censer behind the high altar.

Uncle Werner and Aunt Laura, having opted as usual for a seat neither at the front nor at the back, were halfway down the nave, under the lee of the pulpit. Uncle waved at me, but I pretended not to see him.

It was half-past nine. Miss van Vooren pulled a handle next to the sacristy door; a bell tinkled across the chancel.

Up in the rood loft the choir launched into *God is gone up with a shout, the Lord with the sound of a trumpet.* The priest emerged from the sacristy attended by his acolytes. They gathered a few paces short of the high altar, genuflected, then moved up close to the tabernacle and genuflected again.

I slumped against the back of my seat. All around me the service was unfurling in a panoply of dance, a continuous choreography of outspread arms, bowed heads and incantations that had been going on since goodness knows when, in this very place. Well before the existence of the big house, that was certain, well before there had been battlements rising in the distance beyond the roofs of the village, according to Mr Snellaert.

This was to be the last time I was able to lose myself in historical musings at will, just as easily becoming someone else by wrapping myself in an old curtain from the dressing-up trunk in the attic – but I didn't know that then.

The incense was getting to me, and I tried not to look too groggy. Miss van Vooren stood by the door to the sacristy throughout, watching our every move.

The choir sang *We have a strong city: salvation will God appoint for walls and bulwarks.* The altar boys escorted the priest to the pulpit. The congregation rose from their knees and sat down.

Hélène Vuylsteke exchanged her kneeler for one of the comfortable chairs, but not the tall one which was traditionally reserved for the lord of the manor.

From on high the priest announced to his flock that the contents of this week's collection box would go to the Papal Mission Association. Then he embarked on his sermon, and within two minutes the nave of the church was rolling amid green meadows, much as the disciples had done on the choppy Sea of Galilee when the Saviour walked on water to save them.

'Now don't expect me to do the same,' concluded the priest, and beneath him lips curved into smiles, even though everyone had heard his little joke umpteen times.

A glow of satisfaction travelled down my spine. All was well. The minute hand of some great clock had shifted exactly in time with the measures of the world, everything fitted and all existence was simply there, running neither fast nor slow. I let myself drift along on the current of pre-ordained moves until the Communion was over and Miss van Vooren snapped her fingers.

The youths jumped to their feet. I trailed after them to the sacristy, where the canopy awaited us. It was heavier than I expected.

We carried it to the prearranged spot in the nave, just in front of the altar.

'Just take a small step outwards now,' said Miss van Vooren.

My fellow bearers did as they were told, causing the canopy to unfold overhead.

The priest descended the altar steps holding aloft the monstrance, in which the Sacred Host formed the centre of a sunburst surmounted by two putti bearing a crown.

'Go for it. Not too fast now,' the priest muttered, taking his position under the canopy.

From the aisles came the churchwardens holding candlesticks with lighted candles.

'He is my refuge and my fortress; my God,' sang the choir as they came down from the rood loft to wait for the others by the portal.

The column began to move. I had some trouble keeping up.

'Attaboy,' Uncle whispered to me as we moved past the pulpit, and Aunt wiped a tear from her eye.

The doors of the main entrance swung open. A brilliant wave of sunlight broke over us, bringing a rush of hot air from outside. Behind us the congregation began leaving their pews to bring up the rear of the procession.

'Get on with it, mate,' hissed the boy beside me. The two of us were holding the back poles of the canopy. 'Come on, keep up . . .'

'Shush, lads, shush. No arguing,' muttered the priest, without turning his head.

We proceeded through the churchyard where the graves lay baking in the sun, past the headstone from which my smiling father gazed straight through us into the void.

The almshouse biddies were all in their front gardens, where tables had been set up with bunches of lilac and statues of saints. They clicked their rosaries in Morse code, they knelt for the Holy Sacrament and crossed themselves as we passed, making good the rent for the next year.

We continued past the fields and then along the railway embankment, where the meadow sloped down to the stream. The choir walking some distance ahead of us rang out in double descant: *Lord who goes with us and strikes water from the rocks.*

'Get a move on, Alderweireldt, get a move on,' hissed the tall boy ahead of me. 'Or we'll mess up the formation.'

'They can wait,' said the priest, to reassure me. The muscles in my upper arm and in my wrist were turning numb. Sweat trickled down my back.

The column shuffled to a halt by the entrance to the chapel of the new cemetery, which was surrounded by a row of freshly planted cedars.

'You're doing fine . . .' Uncle Werner murmured from somewhere behind me.

I nodded, but was glad for the chance to rest the base of the pole on the ground while the priest went inside.

It did not happen until we were almost back at the church. We had to stop and wait for a car to turn around because the driver had ignored the gamekeeper's whistle up the road.

My mind must have gone blank. I heard the boy beside me fulminate: 'Alderweireldt, watch out! Eyes as big as saucers, and blind as a bat — Alderweireldt!'

Only then did I notice that the others had started moving again, and I found myself lurching forward to right my end of the canopy with my pole, which consisted of two sections. The upper section was tipping forward at an alarming angle, and the next thing I knew it shot free from the base.

This sent me reeling backwards, and I fell against

someone's legs. I scrambled to my feet amid horrified consternation.

The tall boy had tried to catch my pole but had not been able to stop it thudding against the back of the priest's head.

I saw our shepherd stagger and something flying through the air. The gold crown in the monstrance had come loose. It bounced off the asphalt and under the tall boy's foot, without him noticing, so that he tripped on it and flailed his arms wildly to keep his balance.

Miss van Vooren shot forward to steady him, then snatched up the crown from the verge and fumbled it back into place. She threw me a murderous look.

Uncle retrieved the top half of my pole and reinserted it in the base.

'Worse things happen at sea,' he offered.

After that he stayed at my side, helping me to hold the pole upright. I kept my head down all the rest of the way, convinced that a thousand eyes were fixed on me.

In the sacristy there was a mortal hush. Miss van Vooren was applying a small poultice to the priest's neck.

'That was some fine mess you got us into,' he said.

I was relieved he did not sound too angry.

'I told you he was far too young,' Miss van Vooren said crossly.

'His pa used to do so well . . .' said the priest.

'His pa . . .' she echoed. She breathed heavily down her nostrils, then began to help the shepherd out of his surplice.

We stood in the corner dragging our vestments over our heads.

'If we don't get our money,' the tall boy snarled at me, 'I'll smash your face in, you idiot.'

One of his mates pointed to the sacristy closet, the doors of which were open. He poked the tall boy with his elbow, indicating the shelves with repeated jerks of his head.

'You be the lookout,' the tall boy hissed at me. His hands disappeared into the closet.

'Watch out for those two,' muttered the other boy.

They hadn't noticed a thing. Miss van Vooren was too busy helping the priest to disrobe.

A cork popped softly at my back. I heard the tall boy taking great gulps. One of his friends whispered: 'Give over, my turn now . . .'

There was a scuffle.

'What are you boys up to?' boomed the priest from afar.

'Quick,' hissed one of the boys.

I felt the fumble of hands against my shoulder and found myself hugging a bottle of communion wine.

The others pulled their most innocent faces.

I turned round to find Miss van Vooren glaring at me.

'I might have guessed,' she said, in a rage so cold as to frost my lashes with ice crystals. 'Taking after your father, I do believe.'

When I got home the relations were already drinking their aperitifs under the apple trees. Uncle had dragged the dining table outside. Aunt was in the kitchen putting the soup in the blender.

'Well I never! Here's our acrobat!' cried a cousin of Aunt's. 'Catch a bit of circus fever last night, did you?'

'Lay off him,' said Uncle, 'he's had a rough time.'

I sat down, made myself small, shrinking from their presence like a hedgehog curling up in its nest.

They were good-natured folk. The women had big, blotchy arms bulging out of their sleeveless dresses, and by their second glass of port pink blotches began to appear on their cheeks too.

'One sip and I see double,' cooed Aunt's eldest sister. 'So many people here all of a sudden.' There were guffaws in the background. 'You've got a twin sitting right next to you,' she went on, squinting at me. 'Alike as two peas.'

The afternoon wore on. Roast chickens were carved and stewed pears ladled out with lashings of syrup. A numinous hush descended on the table.

At about three, when half the company had gone out into the road to watch the cycle race go by, a car pulled up in front of the house. Aunt had just started cutting the cakes. High heels tapped sharply across the cobbles in the back yard.

I drew my head in as far as it would go.

'Look, Joris! A visitor for you,' called Uncle.

I twisted round in my chair and saw ankle straps with glittery studs, the deep tan of her legs, the vibrant pink of her dress, the pearls at her throat, and then the thick locks of hair by her cheekbones, just like in her wedding picture.

'Hello, Joris,' she said, smiling. 'Aren't you glad to see me?'

I gazed up into her grey eyes, grey like mine.

'Hello, Ma,' I said.

THEY WOULD NOT STAY LONG, NO LONGER THAN COURTESY required.

'Take a seat, take a seat!' cried Uncle.

His heartiness sounded a mite too enthusiastic to convince me.

The aunts stopped cooing. My mother's brother took a seat near Uncle Werner's cousins, who were discussing their homing pigeons. Their voices trailed off, and they sat with their elbows on their knees studying the grass at their feet, at a loss for a topic of conversation that might appeal to the city type in black shirt and gold-rimmed sunglasses, whose pointy calfskin ankle boots gave off the sweet smell of shoe polish when he swung one leg over the other.

He drew a metal case from his breast pocket, snapped it open in the palm of his hand and, with an overly genteel flourish, offered the cousins a cigarette, for which they stammered their thanks.

They were country folk, sometime farmers who now held jobs or ran small businesses as Uncle did, but they had never quite uprooted themselves from the land that had been ploughed by generation upon generation of their forebears. Ungainly men, gnarled like pollard willows by a boyhood of hard graft on farms, where the odour of the stables mingled with their sweat as they slept, where hens clucked beneath the window and the clock in the hallway ticked away on its rounds of days punctuated by the clatter of pails and churns.

My mother, who had seated herself at my side, draped her arm over the back of my chair. I edged forward, wary of her dizzying nearness and the floaty, almost gravity-defying manner in which she moved and spoke.

'Sponge or Saint-Honoré?' enquired Aunt, indicating the cakes.

She opted for the sponge.

'They're both very light,' Aunt assured her, for she was rather proud of her Saint-Honoré, which consisted of cream puffs piled into a pyramid. 'I used low-fat cream, and marge in place of butter.'

'Sponge,' repeated my mother, 'I'd prefer the sponge.'

'I say, Werner, there's been some news about the head-stone,' said her brother, emitting a cloud of smoke which drifted off over his shoulder towards the chicken run. 'Remind me to fill you in before we go.'

He held the stub of his cigarette between nicotine-stained fingers and raised it to his mouth. His features twisted briefly into a scowl, which was all the more impressive for the dark sunglasses and the pencil moustache pleating like a concertina as he inhaled.

Uncle nodded. 'Will do.'

They must have been in touch with her some time earlier, without my knowledge. They had not called me as they normally did when they had her on the phone, for me to say hello to her in some far-off place and to hear her reply while the line hummed and crackled, as if there were stars imploding in the immeasurable distance separating us during our halting exchange, or long-tailed comets zipping over the Pyrenees.

It was always a relief to be able to pass the receiver to Uncle or Aunt and just stand there listening to the rest of the conversation, even if it was only half of it, for it was the half that was familiar to me. Usually I would hear Aunt telling her I was still eating well, but that I was a bit of a rascal at school.

Once I heard Aunt say, 'Measles? What measles? An epidemic, you say? But he had it five years ago, Francine. You can't get measles twice, you know.'

One of Aunt's sisters asked my mother how she was getting on in Spain. My mother concentrated on cutting her slice of cake with the side of her fork, pretending not to hear.

Her brother blew out a cloud of smoke and said: 'Spain's finished.'

An uncomfortable silence ensued.

'Joris,' said my mother, 'come here with your face, will you.'

She took a dainty handkerchief smelling of violets and brushed the crumbs from the corners of my mouth.

Aunt began to clear the table, making more clatter than

usual as she collected spoons and forks on top of the stack of used plates.

'Can I help?' offered my mother, rising.

'Not to worry,' said Aunt Laura.

My mother sat down again, laid her arm over the back of my chair as before and trailed her fingers over my shoulder from time to time while the table talk continued.

When I went up to my room afterwards, she was there. I had seen her from halfway up the stairs, standing beside my bed and glancing about the room, at the furniture, the walls, almost as if she had stepped into a picture gallery that held little interest for her.

No doubt she had been to the bathroom. Her bag hung on her arm. The suitcase from under my bed was on my writing table. She must have put it there, because I had not touched it for days. The lid was open, and the binoculars had been taken out and placed on my chair. As I reached the top of the stairs I saw her bending over the suitcase. I heard her sigh, with what seemed to me a mixture of sadness and amusement.

'Did you collect all these things yourself?' she asked when I came in.

'I've kept all your postcards, too,' I replied sheepishly, and hated the sound of my voice.

For the next few minutes we stood side by side, heads bowed over the suitcase. I saw myself as a small child in a cotton sunbonnet, sitting beside her on a cloth spread out on a riverbank, gnawing at a crust with my milk teeth.

I tottered down a road between her and my father, clinging on to their hands, I dug holes in the earth with toy spades in the garden at the back of a house of which I had only the dimmest memories.

I stirred the photos with my hand.

She sat down on the edge of the bed, having carefully smoothed her skirt over the back of her thighs with both hands. 'Why don't you sit here with me for a bit? Come on . . .' she said, patting the mattress beside her.

I made her wait while I took one of the elastic bands I used for keeping the photos in place and twisted it round and round my index finger until the tip turned blue.

'Come on . . .' she repeated.

I sat down, released the elastic and savoured the tingling sensation as the blood returned to my fingertip.

'Joris, look at me for once . . .'

It was hard not to return her smile, that huge, glorious smile which sometimes lit up her whole face.

The first hint of crow's feet appeared about her eyes. She must have been in her early thirties at the time. I noticed that she was wearing make-up. It was thinly applied then, but in later years the stuff would be slapped on her face and throat in ever greater quantities, until in the end she became a doll, wrinkle-free and plasticised.

'What did you do in Spain, then?' I asked.

I saw a shadow pass over her irises. She turned her face to the window.

'Nothing very sensible,' she said after a pause.

She looked at me again, rested her hand on my shoulder and stroked my earlobe with her fingers.

'I'd like it if you came to live with me again. You'll be going to a new school a few months from now, anyway. There are good schools in town, your uncles went there too. You can stay with us, our place is far too big for just your uncle and me. You'd have all the space in the world . . .'

She waited for me to reply. I stripped the elastic band off my finger and stuffed it in my pocket.

'I'd really like you to be with me. You can come back here as often as you like. I know you like it here, and that they take good care of you.'

'I'll ask them . . .' I said.

She stood up and adjusted the strap of her shoulder bag.

'They already know. You deserve a good school, that's what they said.'

I did not react.

She cupped my face with her hands. 'I've missed you, Joris. I've really missed you.'

I shut my eyes to avoid meeting hers.

Her lips brushed my forehead, then she was gone.

I heard her going down the stairs. Later on, when they were leaving, I looked out of my window and saw her in the churchyard. She was standing by my father's grave, clutching her shoulder bag, unsteady on her high heels in the coarse gravel.

Her brother was waiting with the engine running.

'Francine,' he called.

She picked her way daintily to the kerb and got in the car.

The dark was setting in and Aunt was in the kitchen finishing the washing-up. Uncle was outside feeding the chickens.

I posted myself in the doorway and stared at her blankly. When it came to getting on her nerves I knew every trick in the book.

The dishcloth flew faster and faster over the pans, as I was pleased to note. She slammed the doors of the kitchen cupboards. She took the already washed tureen and rinsed it again by mistake.

Then she flung the sponge in the sink and turned to confront me.

'Joris! What's the matter with you?'

I shrugged and pulled a face. 'So I'm supposed to be leaving then, am I?'

'Leaving, leaving, who told you that? She wants you to be with her during the week, so you can go to school there. That's all.'

She returned to her pans.

'Well, perhaps it's time to move on . . .'

'I want to stay here.'

'It's not up to you.'

She paused in her scouring, took a deep breath and fixed her eyes on the cupboard door over the draining board.

'Whichever way you look at it, she's still your ma, Joris.

We can't stop her. But it's early days yet, plenty of time for you to get used to the idea . . .'

She set the pan on the drying-rack.

'And us too.'

'I'm going up to bed,' I said.

She offered her cheek for me to kiss her good-night, but I stalked out of the kitchen.

The next morning I woke up late. I had slept soundly, and was not conscious of having dreamed. Last night before getting into bed I had closed the lid on my father's suitcase and slid it back where it belonged.

From my bed I surveyed my room. I willed each crack meandering across the ceiling to imprint itself on my memory, so that when I was packed off to that stuffy town house just shutting my eyes would be enough to whisk me back to the comfort of my old bedroom.

Aunt called from downstairs. She asked me to put something clean on because she was taking me to Hélène Vuylsteke's for coffee at the big house. I could go out and play in the grounds if I liked, she said, no lack of space there.

She sent me back upstairs twice, the first time because the jumper I was wearing was too tight and the second because it was too loose.

We set out a little after midday, and were to call at Miss van Vooren's on the way, as she had also been invited.

Despite the overgrown cedars screening the walls of her house, Miss van Vooren had not been spared the heat. She opened the front door looking rather flustered, shook hands with Aunt and glared at me as if I were some small dead rodent the cat had deposited on the doorstep.

'Could you wait a moment,' she said. 'I still have to do my hair, and I need to take something for my ulcer before we go.'

We were not shown into the parlour, where she usually kept me waiting while she composed her list of groceries, but into a rarely used antechamber on the opposite side of the hall. When Aunt sat down, the springs of her chair squealed as though in fright.

On the mantelpiece stood dreary little bunches of dried flowers between framed photographs of prim young ladies in front of churches, basilicas, and every Virgin's grotto in the area. They were invariably disposed around the central figure of Miss van Vooren, who wore a look of permanent migraine and sometimes linked arms with Hélène.

'I must be up there somewhere too, with all the rest,' said Aunt.

A musty odour hung in the room. The walls were obviously affected by rising damp, which the seldom-lit stove did nothing to combat.

'God, what a pong in here!' I said, in a much louder voice than usual. Miss van Vooren had left the door to the hall ajar. Elsewhere in the house she turned a tap on. Secretly I hoped she had heard me. The incident in the sacristy was still fresh in my memory.

'Joris!' Aunt remonstrated, holding her forefinger to her lips.

'Well, you said so yourself! She may be pure in spirit,

but her cupboards could do with a dusting . . . that's what you said – I heard you.'

'That's quite enough . . .'

'Even Uncle says so. Smells as musty in her house as between a nun's legs, he says.'

Aunt stood up, grabbed me by my arm and sat me down on the chair beside her.

'What's the matter with you today? I'll send you straight home if you don't mind your tongue.'

I was fuming.

Just as I opened my mouth for an even ruder rejoinder, Miss van Vooren appeared in the hallway. With her dark glasses on and a filmy little headscarf reining in her swollen hairdo except for a curl on either side, she looked more or less her old self. All she needed was a pair of glass wings for her to look exactly like an insect whose frail appearance belied a nasty sting.

'All set now,' she said.

Aunt and I stood up and followed her out of the house.

We walked up the tree-lined alleyway to the back entrance of the estate. Miss van Vooren had no objection. The main access was on the other side: a formal gateway with posts of classical design crowned by urns and horns of plenty, the aesthetic effect of which Miss van Vooren considered wasted on ordinary folk.

With each step we took in the knee-high grass between the lindens, the throbbing activity of the village dwindled away behind the banks of brushwood curving around the estate like defensive earthworks. The afternoon took on a compacted stillness, rent now and then by the shrieks of peacocks in the trees.

Before us sprawled the big house, bathed in sunshine. The awning had been erected over the terrace. We shut the gate behind us, and as we crossed the footbridge a figure in a wide-brimmed straw hat came down the steps towards us.

'Welcome, all three of you!' exclaimed Hélène Vuylsteke. 'How nice to see you, Rosa.'

Kisses were exchanged.

'And our celestial acrobat too . . .' she smirked.

'The talk of the village, he is,' Miss van Vooren said offhandedly.

'Oh come now, Rosa,' laughed Hélène Vuylsteke. 'Nous deux, nous avons survécu deux guerres. After what we've been through, that kind of upset is a mere bagatelle.'

Miss van Vooren's eyebrow raised itself over the rim of her sunglasses.

Hélène ushered us up the steps.

'Monsieur said we were free to use the terrace. Enjoy the fine weather, he said, because you never know how long it will last. Especially at his age. Après la pluie vient la pluie – that's what he says nowadays.'

On the terrace beneath the awning stood a table laden with a mass of china and silver; the sight of it caused Aunt to catch her breath. The girl was sitting a little way along, playing with her dolls. She had laid her own table, much lower than the other and surrounded by all her favourites propped on miniature wicker chairs. Halfway down the plastic ears of the largest of her dolls, a fair-haired beauty in a satin dress, sat the crown which the clairvoyant had presented to her at the circus.

'Isabeau, nos invités sont arrivés,' said Hélène Vuylsteke.

The girl sauntered over the terrace towards Aunt, shook her hand and curtsyed prettily. She repeated the ritual with Miss van Vooren, but when it was my turn she merely said 'Oh, bonjour' with an almost imperceptible nod at me, and returned to her dolls.

'Sa propre famille,' Hélène Vuylsteke said in a placatory tone. 'They won't let her out of their sight ...'

She invited us to sit down, and proceeded to pour coffee. I could see my face idiotically distorted in the silver coffeepot when she filled my cup. In the centre of the table glistened two strawberry cakes layered with transparent jelly.

'Cut the cake for us, will you, Rosa,' said Hélène.

The girl was served her portion on a separate platter which she carried to her assembly of dolls, where she divided it among four toy plates.

A lively conversation ensued on that side of the terrace, in the course of which the girl put on a different voice for each of her playmates.

At our table Hélène conversed primarily with Miss van Vooren, rattling away in a French that I could tell Aunt was at pains to follow. She was not at ease.

'Enjoy your cake did you, Joris?' she asked, in an attempt to feel she was part of it all.

'Yes, Aunt. I'm mad about strawberries.'

I looked out over the lawn stretching towards the pond. A peacock with fanned tail-feathers stepped out from the undergrowth and went in pursuit of a hen. Further off, among the stands of trees, the dew of the past night lingered in damp veils between the bundles of hay, swathing the view in a bluish haze that brought the world to a standstill. Even the swans gliding almost imperceptibly on the pond settled their long necks back to rest between their wings.

At the end of the alleyway the tower clock struck three, followed almost immediately at our backs by a low rumble of mechanisms gearing up all over the house, as if an immense swarm of butterflies were fluttering up from the cellars. Above the rumble, at intervals of a few seconds, clocks began to chime with neurotic urgency in one room after another. There were tinkly tunes, and also a grandfather clock conducting the orchestra, which seemed to be moving through the premises from south to north for a full half-minute before dying away in the distance.

'Our Marie,' said Hélène, smiling. She must have noted the surprise on our faces. 'She's getting on in years. When she adjusts the clocks in the house she forgets she's not quite as nimble on her feet as she used to be. There's at least a minute's difference between one end of the house and the other.'

She gazed out over the park. 'Time passes, passes,' she sighed. 'Je trouve ces bois d'une tristesse . . .'

'Oh yes, trees can make one very sad,' said Aunt, determined to contribute to the conversation.

'Tous ces arbres que nous avons vus si petits . . .' mused Hélène. She took a sip of her coffee and seemed lost in thought.

Miss van Vooren coughed. 'I've caught a summer cold,' she said, clearing her throat. 'They're the worst.'

Hélène Vuylsteke noticed my boredom.

'I'll ask Isabella to show you the library,' she said. 'You like reading, do you?'

'Reading?' echoed Aunt. 'He likes nothing better.'

Hélène called the girl and asked her to take me into the house. Isabella gave a distracted sigh. She put down her napkin, stood up and crossed to the french windows of the adjoining salon, which were open. 'En avant, venez avec moi.'

I trailed after her as she crossed the salon to the door opening on to the hall, where a staircase with cool marble steps curved upwards beside concave walls. Above the plaster mouldings a host of Van Callants gazed down at me, row upon row of them in gilt picture frames reaching all the way up to the ceiling. They were dressed according to the fashions of their day, and had taken on a spun-sugar look where the varnish had yellowed.

The girl was already at the top of the stairs. 'Viens, dépêche-toi, ils sont tous morts et pas intéressants . . .'

She ran down the long hallway and stopped at a door at the far end. A dry smell of leather and wood wafted towards me as she pushed it open.

Looking past her I saw books with brown, ridged spines. The light in the room was tempered by partially lowered blinds.

'Entre,' said the girl.

I did so, and the door fell to behind me. She had left me on my own.

I clumped over the floorboards until my footsteps were smothered in ankle-deep carpet. There were two leather armchairs by the hearth, and a half-smoked cigar lay dead in an ashtray on a salver.

All about the room were tables on which rested open books as long as my arm. I went over to look.

On one frontispiece the inscription read '*The Glory of Flanders*', beneath a lion holding the Van Callant escutcheon aloft. I turned the page gingerly, using both hands, and found myself looking at a map upon which, after a moment's scrutiny, I discovered the village, half obscured by a circle of damp. Its name was written as 'Stuvenberga', and I could make out the church, and slightly further up, in a bend of the stream, the original castle with ramparts and gardens laid out in a grid.

On the other side of the table lay a volume even bigger than all the others. It was an atlas open at a page showing a map of the world with continents in many colours, as garish as a parrot's feathers, and an inscription in fancy lettering: *Recens et Integra – Orbit Descriptio*.

I recognised France and Spain. The shapes were familiar, but here their coastlines jutted far more raggedly into the ocean than on the wall maps in Mr Snellaert's classroom, as if they had been drawn by a child's unsteady hand, and also the world itself looked more like an apple than a globe. It was flanked by seraphim holding back draperies, which, it seemed, they would let fall when there were no spectators, so as to keep the earth from fading.

I was so engrossed in the map that I was taken completely by surprise when the tabletop juddered. I looked up to find Isabella Van Callant staring into my eyes.

She had climbed on to the table without a thought for the books, and was on her knees facing me. She said nothing, but wore a beatific smile which made me very nervous.

I dropped my eyes and, for want of something to do, made to turn the page with the map of the world. Just as I placed my other hand on the facing page to avoid all risk of dog-earing, the girl quickly raised the back cover of the atlas, clapped it shut on my hands and brought both her knees down on top.

My hands were imprisoned.

'Let me go!' I cried.

'Quoi?' she sneered.

She reached out and pulled the hair on my forehead, then grabbed me roughly by the chin.

'Regarde-moi, fermier . . .' she said, bringing her face close to my mine. So close that I could see the brown of her irises flecked with blue and grey and green, shards from all those varnished eyes looking out from the portraits in the stairwell. There were freckles on her nose and on her cheeks.

'Petit de Stuyvenberghe,' she hissed, 'tu es mon pris-
onnier.'

'Laissez-moi,' I wailed. My hands were turning numb
and the edges of the atlas cut painfully into my forearms
under her weight.

She grinned and came even closer. I could feel her
breath on my cheeks.

Suddenly she seized the back of my head with both
hands and pulled me to her.

Her lips squelched against mine. It was utterly revolting,
and I nearly gagged at the sourish taste of her darting
tongue while her breath howled in my ears.

She let go of me, drew back a little and regarded me
with grim triumph in her brown eyes.

My chin was wet with her saliva and I couldn't wipe it
off.

The girl leaned forward again. I tried to duck my head.

'Et maintenant,' she said hoarsely, 'une petite excursion
aux forêts de l'équateur . . .'

Her right hand slid down over my shirt to my stomach,
then groped under my clothes for my navel, which she
fondled. Fixing me with her eyes, she wriggled her fingers
under the waistband of my trousers.

'Stop it, please,' I squeaked.

I was even more terrified when she stirred her hand
around my groin.

'Ton petit bâtiment n'est pas très fort,' she said. She
sounded surprised.

I tried to wrench myself free, but she was gripping my

shirt with her other hand. When she shifted her buttocks slightly to steady her position, I was able to work one of my hands loose from the book.

The girl wobbled precariously, her knees still pressing down on the book, while I flailed my arm. I caught hold of her hair, tightened my fist, yanked her head down as far as it would go.

Yelping with pain, she snatched her hand out of my trousers, grabbed my arm and sank her teeth into my wrist, using her other hand to claw my cheek.

I screwed up my eyes so hard that the tears beaded out at the corners. Neither of us would let go.

I don't know how long we were locked together like that, spluttering to stifle our pain. Suddenly the pressure of her knees on my pinioned hand lifted. There was a loud crack and then a thud.

The binding of the book had split open along the spine, causing the girl to slide off the table on to the carpet amid a flurry of loose sheets.

She scrambled to her feet, looking dazed. For a moment we stood there glaring at each other, speechless, she with her hair dishevelled, me with my shirt tails out of my trousers.

Then she started screaming: 'Tu es horrible, et toute ta famille! Your father drank himself to death! The whole world knows about it, except you, you're a cretin . . .'

Knees shaking, I stuffed my shirt into my trousers, gathered up the pages from the carpet and stacked them as neatly as I could on the table. Then I put them back between the covers, to hide the damage. The girl ranted on.

'He ruined his liver. He stank to high hell, and so do you. He's so full of alcohol that he can't even rot in his tomb . . . Ma bonne m'a dit. C'est déguelasse.'

'Non!' I burst out. And before I knew it I had taken a swipe at her.

She was astounded.

'T'es maigre comme un clou,' she scoffed.

A moment later the door opened and in came Hélène Vuylsteke. Directing her gaze from me to the girl and back again, she padded across the carpet towards us with icy calm.

Still fixing me with her eyes, but clearly addressing the girl, she said: 'Ma chère, ne cherchez pas les oranges sous les pommiers . . . Go to the bathroom and comb your hair.'

The girl sauntered past Hélène out of the room.

'Pull yourself together,' said Hélène. She waited for me to straighten my clothes and then marched ahead of me down the stairs to the terrace, where Aunt was chatting to Miss van Vooren.

'Were the books nice?' she asked.

'I had to drag him away by force,' said Hélène, with a smile in which only I recognised the venom.

We left at about five.

'Till next time,' said Hélène, all smiles as she shook my hand. 'I'll give Isabella your regards then, shall I?'

*

'You're shaking,' said Aunt as we reached the end of the alleyway.

'I think I'm coming down with something,' I said.

'A summer cold, probably,' said Miss van Vooren. 'It's the time of year, I expect. You want to be careful, it can turn into bronchitis . . .'

'It'll pass,' I said.

I ran home ahead of them, down the church lane. I slipped past Uncle serving customers in the shop and shut myself up in my room for the rest of the evening.

AUGUST WAS UPON US. AT HOME NO ONE SPOKE OF MY impending departure. It was as if there were sheets hanging to dry from all the rafters, blotting every sound in the house.

'It's not as bad as you think,' said Aunt, noticing my troubled look. 'You can come over every weekend if you like. We've agreed on that.'

I looked at Uncle. He hunched his shoulders and gave me a soothing smile.

'There's not much we can do about it,' he said, adding, 'and even if there were, we mightn't want to.'

He could see I was confused by his remark. He took a deep breath and glanced at Aunt, who was snipping the football forecast out of the newspaper. She always taped it to the pane in the shop door.

'We'll be right here,' she said. 'We're not going anywhere. Where would we go, anyway? We'll always be here. It'll do you good, you know. More than you think.'

I tried protesting in the only way I could think of. Several days before the fifteenth of the month, the date I was to be fetched, I got the suitcase out from under my bed and put it on my table.

First I just left it there, wide open. Perhaps I hoped the accusatory sight of it would be enough to give Aunt a stab of guilt each time she went past my room.

In the next day or two I began to empty it out, trying to make up my mind what to take with me and what to leave behind. It was important to leave sufficient items behind for me to feel homesick about. There were plenty of photos that I slipped like so many banknotes between the pages of Aunt's album, as if I were entrusting my father to a foster family. But I did set aside a handful, which I tied with an elastic band, to take with me, along with my father's school exercise book which Uncle had given me ages ago and which I treasured because I was modelling my handwriting and my signature on his at the time.

I tipped all my mother's letters into a drawer and left them there, because I knew Aunt would be annoyed when she found them. ,

There was no need to pack any clothes. 'You'll be needing smart outfits for that new school of yours. From now on she can buy them herself,' Aunt said tartly. There was a sharp edge to her voice whenever she mentioned my mother which always made me feel awkward.

I tried not to count off the remaining days. In those final weeks I felt I was sleepwalking, quite devoid of any sense of volition, and that there were hands in the dead of night untying my shoelaces, grabbing my ankles, wrenching the shoes from my feet, undoing the buttons on my shirt, shaking my limp arms out of my sleeves and scattering flowers on my pillow.

Outside, August was rounding off the summer, allowing the first inklings of winter to rise from the ground as the evenings wore on. In the weeks following the annual fair the churchyard had begun to sprout wooden posts next to some of the gravestones, with notices stapled to them furnished with impressive stamps and signatures not half as neat as my father's, and puzzling phrases like 'legislation enforceable under section such and such' and 'in compliance with regulations governing groundwater levels', as if the dead were in danger of drowning down there, and these were distress signals in their hour of peril.

Someone had marked several of the graves, including my father's, with a bright red dot. I didn't dare take a closer look. I was afraid I would get all emotional and start kicking the side of the bluestone slab or hammering my fists on that inane grin curving his lips in the oval portrait screwed above his name.

I managed to keep my mouth shut for about five days. Then one evening, when Aunt resolutely ignored my long face, I finally burst out with: 'I know.'

They both stopped eating. 'What do you know?' Uncle asked.

'I just know, that's all,' I replied.

Aunt put down her spoon, pushed back her chair and clapped her hands on her thighs. She looked at Uncle. He looked back.

'People talk a lot of rubbish,' he said.

I cut up my slice of bread as reproachfully as I could.

'Just like your father,' he growled. 'If you've got something on your mind, kiddo, you could at least open your mouth and say so. Can't tell what's wrong by the smell, can we?'

I scraped the bottom of my bowl of buttermilk pudding over and over with my spoon. I knew exactly how to wind them up.

'Can I have some more sugar?' I asked casually.

'You know where it's kept,' snapped Aunt.

I got up and went through to the scullery.

'It was his stomach that killed him, Joris,' said Aunt when I sat down again. 'That's all you need to know. They saw no point in an operation. He couldn't keep anything down at the end. Had his bed in there.' She pointed to the front room.

'She couldn't handle it, your mamma couldn't. You should have seen the state of you when you first got here . . .'

'Laura,' said Uncle Werner. 'Please, don't . . .'

There was no stopping her.

'Dammit, your hair was full of stale breadcrumbs, three days old at least.'

She picked up her spoon. 'I was the one changing his sheets, nobody else. Me and Werner, that is. Three times a day, sometimes, when he spat blood. Spat out all his insides in the end.'

She bent over her bowl and ate. Then she put down her spoon again. 'So now you know.'

I got up and made for the door.

'Joris,' Uncle called after me.

'Leave me alone.'

'They never liked us,' I overheard Aunt say.

'Nor we them, Laura,' said Uncle.

A short time afterwards he came upstairs and sat down on the edge of my bed.

'Yes, my boy,' he sighed. 'She's going through the change. So are you, in a way . . . And then there's me, the dumbo in between.'

His chest shook with rueful laughter. Me going through a change, what could he mean? He could have been my father. What if, in the days before I was born, he had gone to one of those parties now fossilised in the stiff pages of the albums, and had asked my mother to dance? If that had happened, my real father would simply have been some strange uncle, the kind of relation who was remembered at family gatherings with shakes of the head and remarks about what a shame it was to go so young.

In photos dating from before my birth, my absence from them felt like an unforgivable oversight. There was something wrong about the sunlight, and about the smiling faces at dinners from which I was excluded. Not only was it impossible to imagine the world without me in it, the question whether I would still be me if my mother had married someone else kept preying on my mind. Who was I? Which part of me came from where?

When I took a good look at Uncle I saw a sort of mirror

image of myself, a portrait that the artist had taken a lot of liberties with, so that I could see the likeness in the features while the eyes were those of a complete stranger. I hated his complacency, because I knew I had it in me too, deep down. The boys I jostled when we stood in line at school always made me pity them for one reason or another: their trousers were too short or their pullovers were their brothers' cast-offs or they were hopeless at arithmetic, or just because I happened to be me and there was nothing, nothing at all, to be done about it.

'There is so much we don't know,' said Uncle, as if he could read my thoughts. 'Your pa, my brother, Joris... Don't forget I slept in the same bed with him for eighteen years in this very house...'

He paused, letting his shoulders sag.

'She thought she could wean him off it, I suppose... Perhaps I thought so too... He was headstrong, you know. A bit bashful at first perhaps... Once he got going, though... always first in line. Charging ahead... And then...'

He put his arm around my shoulders. I wanted to snuggle up to him, but thought that would be childish.

'I don't know why... But so it goes, that's all I can say. So it goes. The older I get, the less I understand... But perhaps you'll be able to explain it to me, later on, when you're grown up and have read many more books.'

He slapped his hand on my knee and stood up. At the door he turned round.

'Our ma made us go out to work at seventeen. Work

and save money, that was what we were supposed to do. When I get too old for hard graft, she used to say, you two can have the shop.'

He stepped into the corridor, leaving my door open. 'A good woman . . . far too good,' he muttered. The rest of the evening passed in a silence so fragile that the slightest disturbance made a din. In the scullery Aunt emptied the cupboards so as to clean the insides, which gave her ample opportunity to rattle pots and pans and jam jars by way of Morse signals of reproach to the rest of the house. Finally the whistle of the boiling kettle brought salvation.

'Anyone for tea?' she called, in token of truce.

I returned the book to Mr Snellaert on my last day. I had spotted his bicycle in the school playground, and the steel door to the hallway and the classrooms beyond was open.

There was no reply when I knocked. It was some time before he called for me to come in.

It was dark in the room. He had lowered the blinds over the big south-facing window. The sun coming in through the slits cast thin horizontal stripes across the desks, lighting up the triangles and protractors which were normally kept on top of the blackboard but which had been washed and now lay drying amid the sharp smell of detergent.

From the far end of the classroom, next to the stove, came the whirr of a film projector.

'Mr Snellaert?' I said.

A cupboard door closed.

'Ah it's you, Alderweireldt...'

Something stirred at the back of the room. The blinds rattled softly and the stripes of sunlight widened. There he stood, in the corner at the back, by what had been my desk for the entire school year. Over the noticeboard hung long ribbons made of something resembling dark plastic.

'I was busy with my cine films,' he said, not seeming to mind being disturbed.

Mr Snellaert's hobby was common knowledge. He would turn up with his film camera on special occasions such as friendly football matches or village fairs, and it was funny how everyone gave their hair a quick pat or straightened their collar as soon as the lens swung in their direction.

'That's the trouble,' I had heard him remark one day. 'The moment they know they're being filmed, half of it's ruined.'

He showed his films as entertainment during village festivities, and gave his compilations titles like 'Customs and Crafts of Yore', or 'Forgotten Characters'. The volleys of laughter and cries of recognition from behind the drawn curtains of the parish hall would be audible in the road outside. He always addressed his audience as Dear Friends.

'I've come to return the book,' I said. 'I'm leaving tomorrow.'

He made his way among the desks towards me.

'So I've heard. I hope you'll keep your nose a bit cleaner over there. You'll find life in the city very different.'

My last school report had not been brilliant, just average.

'Could do very much better if he tried,' had been his final comment under the heading 'General Attitude'.

'Oh well, perhaps you've learned a thing or two from that book.'

'Yes, sir.'

He took the book from me and tapped the spine with his fingers as he walked to the cupboard at the back of the classroom to put it back with the others.

'Perhaps it's a good thing you're going away. Things seem to be going downhill faster than ever . . .' he said, more to himself than to me.

He slipped the book in where it belonged. 'There's a sequel. *Mysteries of Civilisation.* Would you care to read it?'

'I don't know when I can bring it back,' I replied.

He had already taken the hefty volume from the shelf. 'You'll come over from time to time, won't you? Besides, if you promise it'll be in good hands,' he said, handing me the book, 'I might turn forgetful.'

I could not see his face clearly in the dimness, but I knew he was grinning.

'Thank you,' I said.

'Shame I didn't bring my camera to the procession the other Sunday,' he said, crossing to the projector. 'I did have it with me later on, for the bicycle race, but by then I'd missed the high point of the day . . .'

I felt the blood rush to my cheeks, and hoped he didn't notice.

'Otherwise I could have spliced you in after your father. That would have been capital. One acrobat after another.'

He noted my baffled expression.

'Get a chair,' he said, smiling.

I pulled up a chair between the stove and the projector and sat down. Mr Snellaert took some round, flat tins from the table beside him and studied the labels.

'I store my films the way women store jam,' he said. 'Summer 68 . . . Summer 52 . . . Summer . . . Yes, that should be the one.'

He opened the tin and took out something resembling a wheel, which he clicked on to the projector.

'Must take care not to break it, the stuff gets brittle with age.' The wheel was wound round with the same sort of strip that was hanging from the noticeboard.

'What I need is a proper cutting table, really, but the expense . . .' He appeared to be talking to himself, so I held my tongue.

'Right, all set.'

The stripes of sunlight narrowed as the blinds were lowered again. Mr Snellaert pressed a button. The projector threw a beam of light on to the blackboard, over which he had draped a sheet kept in place by three board wipers along the top.

'Now for the show,' said the master, rubbing his hands.

First I saw the stream in black and white, winding among back gardens, some with hedges that were no longer there, and I saw a cow charging across a field to the water's edge, where she dropped to her knees in the grass with a curiously determined air. Abruptly, the screen went dark.

'It still needs a title,' said Mr Snellaert. 'Something like "Wartime Memories", perhaps.'

The screen lit up again and a troupe of boys wearing gumboots stood in the water by the railway embankment, near where the stream discharged from a brick-lined tunnel. They waved. Laughed. The camera zoomed in. Faces were pulled in close-up, and among the jostle of heads and caps I could make out the long handle of a rake or hoe.

'They had a whale of a time,' said the master. 'And so did I, to be honest. I had them find out the names of the German soldiers. They'd gone into hiding when the war ended. The Canadians found all four of them. Hadn't eaten for days. Thin as rakes. Some Master Race! They scratched their names in the cement with their penknives – you can still see them, probably. But nowadays, what with my rheumatism . . .' he patted his hip, 'things aren't as easy as they used to be.'

The antics on screen continued, with much waving of arms and splashing in the stream amid bare knees and rubber boots. There was something unreal about the scene, compounded by the whirr of the projector and intermittent clicks of the reel.

Around someone's shins there appeared, as if by magic, an everted cuff of lacy foam and flying droplets, where-upon the legs shot up from the bed of the stream in a wide arc over the bulrushes and irises until their owner landed on his two feet on the bank.

Mr Snellaert scratched his scalp. He was about to speak when the picture changed.

I saw a pair of muddy hands displaying a couple of dented, rusty shells with trails of duckweed.

'Yes, that's right, we found them in the stream. One of the lads had a rake with him. I had them cleaned. They're over there, on the bookshelf.'

Meanwhile the camera zoomed out, somewhat jerkily. The hands grew wrists, forearms, and then suddenly a chin appeared, and a mouth with a crooked smile I thought looked familiar.

'Now who could that be?' said the master in mock surprise.

It was Uncle Werner. His blond hair stuck out on all sides, just like in the old photos. I recognised his speckled pullover and the collar of his checked shirt. He puffed up his cheeks and rolled his eyes in a squint.

'Always up to mischief,' Mr Snellaert grinned. 'I even locked him in the coal cellar once because he wouldn't stop acting the clown, and things got out of hand.'

I was only half listening. The film was very strange. The figures suddenly moved close together, as if someone had ordered them to stand in a row. Equally suddenly the group of five or six youths switched from peering into the lens to lurching backwards and flapping their arms.

'Drat,' said the master. 'Must've rewound it back to front. I thought it looked a bit odd . . .'

One by one they leaned forward. As though taking their leave from an oriental emperor on whom no back was permitted to be turned, they retreated through the water to the brick mouth of the tunnel. I saw the handle of the rake sink between their heads and blend into the alder coppice.

'Oh bother,' grumbled Mr Snellaert. He made to switch off the projector. 'Silly me.'

'Wait!' I cried.

In the middle of the stream stood my father. Legs wide, hands on hips, water up to his ankles, eyes screwed up against the sun. He brought his hand to his ear, seemingly to hear what the master was saying, then I saw him nod. He bent over and with his hands on his thighs began to move backwards to the dark hole in the railway embankment. He waved again, then crouched, looked around him for the last time, as if he would never see the world again, and was engulfed in darkness.

The image juddered, the film flapped loose from the reel.

'He was the first to come out at the other end,' the master said. 'I remember it well. Never let a chance go by to crawl over or under things . . .'

The master switched off the projector.

'Died far too young, did your pa,' he said.

He walked to the window and pulled up the blinds.

'You make sure you live longer than him.'

I took the book home. *Mysteries of Civilisation.* 'Ziggurat' was the most exciting word in it.

The car arrived at about half-past ten the next morning. They really couldn't stay, they said, too busy. My mother's brother wore his sunglasses and slouched against the car, smoking a cigarette while she went inside to take charge of my suitcase. She said it was very kind but they had stopped on the way for a quick bite on the dike at Blankenberge.

I merely shook hands with Uncle and Aunt – much too formally, I thought.

'See you in a couple of weeks, then,' said Aunt.

They didn't come to the door to wave goodbye, and I didn't look back as we circled the churchyard before turning into the high street and then taking the motorway.

NOW, WHENEVER I THINK BACK TO THOSE EARLY DAYS IN my first nest, and to the years that followed, during which, until the age of sixteen or so, I spent at least two week-ends a month there, I see myself walking alone along the fields, and nearly always it is summer. Encapsulating all my memories like a glass dome is the languid stillness of a day in July. A July of parched mud in the verge, a cat streaking out from under the hedge, and high in the azure sky a sports plane chugging faintly over a world devoid of human life.

The road is deserted. In the upstairs windows above the shop, the net curtains sway gently in the draught. The screen door clicks open and shut, the table is laid, the kettle is still warm on the hob, and up in the gutter pigeons dance the fandango.

My existence there is limited to seeing, hearing, tasting and smelling. When I look in the mirror I can see through myself. Maybe I'm in heaven.

A few days before Uncle Werner died I helped carry him from his sickbed by the window to the table. While Aunt was in the kitchen heating the milk I cut his slice of bread into strips, watched him eat them with tremulous movements and heard him take greedy gulps from the large bowl he held to his mouth with fingers like desiccated wings.

He had turned into an overgrown, hoar-frosted child howling in the night because of his dreams, from which he woke in terror. Using my handkerchief for want of a napkin, I wiped the cream off his upper lip while our eyes met. I saw death in his bewildered gaze, which was something I had only read about in books and which seemed rather far-fetched and sentimental at the time, but I saw it in the whites of his eyes and in his dilated pupils gorging themselves on the living world for as long as they were able.

He only spoke once. 'Joris,' he said. I had a feeling it was more an unconscious reflex at the sight of my face than true recognition, but I responded with 'Pa', anyway.

Aunt sat at a corner of the table and watched, seeking to glean some slight comfort from every sip of milk he took, every morsel of bread, although she knew it was hopeless.

Each time I visited she put her hands on my shoulders and said: 'Still growing, I do believe', whereas it was she who was shrinking in my arms.

I cannot think back to the pair of them without being reminded of my school compositions. Not because of their headings, but because of the illusion that every utterance from those days could still safely be erased. I see myself happily brushing the rubber crumbs off my page, unperturbed by the gouges left in the paper by my sharp pencil.

When we had carried Uncle back from the table to the bed, Aunt said that quite honestly she hoped it would be over soon. It might sound a bit strange to hear someone say this about the person with whom they had shared everything for the past fifty years, but as far as she was concerned it was preferable to be sad about him being dead than about him having to suffer so much in life, such as it was. This was no life, she said, not for him and not for anyone else.

She sat on the chair by the bed in which Uncle lay on his side, his face to the window. Her hands lay on her lap; she wore the nylon flowered apron which, in the old days, she would put on in the kitchen and whip off before sitting down to a meal, but which she seemed to wear all the time nowadays. When Uncle became restless she would automatically put her hand on his arm without interrupting her litany, and rub her thumb over the back of his hand until he quietened down.

I think you could call their marriage a happy one. It had a special aroma, of which I was probably more aware than they ever were. It wafted across my face every day. It lingered in the fibres of the bath towels, it floated over the lavatory when I lifted the seat and could smell their water. They never flushed after a pee, presumably out of thrift, and considered it very affected of me when I started doing it.

They thought that life in the city was to blame, that it was one of those wasteful habits I had picked up from my mother. But I didn't do it because I recoiled from their intimacy, I did it because I wanted to smell my own water. I felt hurt when they called me a townie, even though I knew they meant it kindly.

I was not there when he died and I regret that now. My regret has grown fiercer over the years and at the same time gentler, for regret seems to me to be the guaranteed interest that life pays out in ever more generous instalments. I called his name. He craned his neck and raised his hand in a reflex as I passed the window on my way down the garden to the road. Three days later he was dead.

After the funeral Aunt kept the hospital bed. She was finding it harder and harder to climb the stairs. So every night she left her clothes on the very chair she had sat on during her vigils at Uncle's bedside until his heart gave up, crossed herself, and heaved herself into the bed downstairs.

I did not call very often, and never stayed long enough. I saw her arranging biscuits in a circle on a plate which she sent sliding across the table towards me like a lifebuoy.

'Have another,' I heard her say. 'They'll only go stale otherwise', which was her way of pleading for me not to go just yet.

I don't recall her ever voicing concerns about what state she would be found in, but I do know that last thing at night she never failed to rinse her fork and spoon, set her plate and cup in the drying rack over the sink, hang the towel on its peg on the back of the kitchen door, drape the folded dishcloth over the tap, and moreover that she never failed to put her slippers side by side under the chair before getting into bed. No chance of being caught unawares, the way an unguarded moment is captured on camera.

She died in her sleep, head lolling sideways, newspaper on her lap. I received a phone call from the woman next door who looked in several times a day and whose conversation was larded with the sort of idle gossip I used to overhear in the shop, where the dead littered the conversations like discarded shopping lists.

She had eaten well that afternoon, and had looked well, too, said the woman; she had apparently been dead only a few hours when they found her, and according to the doctor had probably never known, just slipped away. The neighbour had been given my number some while ago in case anything happened, and she told me to look in the top drawer of the dresser. Aunt had left a note there, for the sake of convenience.

'No flowers, Joris,' it read, 'and I want the cheapest coffin. Don't forget to go to the bank. Pay the undertaker with what's in the account and keep the rest for yourself. The notary will see to everything. You can rent out the shop if you like. The roof is still good, only the windows are in bad shape. Your ever loving Aunt Laura. Give my regards to your ma.'

*

The house had long since grown too big for her, for all that it had shrunk to a few downstairs rooms. The shelves in the shop, unused for the last eight years or so, still held an assortment of unsold food tins, and also some bottles of liqueur, which had turned to sugar. Now and then when I visited she would open one, making the crystals crunch under the screw top.

Practically every drawer I looked in contained old savings stamps, forgotten coupons, bits of string, corks, all the bits and bobs she always stored away because you never knew when they might come in handy.

The wardrobe upstairs was still filled with their clothes. Uncle's bowler hat, the only remnant of his wedding outfit, still lay on the shelf, and from a hanger swayed a clear plastic shroud containing Aunt's coat with the fur collar, her only smart outer garment, which she was so anxious to keep in pristine condition that one day, during Mass, in the sanctified hush of the consecration, a single stray mothball dropped out of the lining and bounced away over the flagstones. She pretended not to notice, although she paled.

An antique dealer was interested in the counters and display cabinets. I told him he could take everything if he cleared out the rest of the house as well. All I kept were the albums and a malachite paperweight, which I don't recall seeing anywhere but on the edge of Aunt's dressing table, and never holding down papers or envelopes.

I came upon the box she kept their love letters in, an

old chocolate box tied with a ribbon, but the letters had gone. Aunt must have torn them up, or burned them. As a boy I never dared to snoop in that box, for fear that the satin paper lining would rustle all too accusingly if I raised the lid. No one will ever know what they wrote in those letters, but I can imagine the stilted expressions of their affection without having read them.

Why is it always the letters people burn when they want to have a go at rewriting – or editing – their history? Why is it so seldom the photos that get thrown away? The festive gathering, the outings, the everyday snapshots, all those slivers of light rescued from oblivion by the dry click of a camera. All those images of people, young and old, fresh-faced or careworn, all the commotion, the laughter, the long faces, the dreamy looks, the vacant stares – why are they perceived to be less damning than words inked on paper?

Sometimes I wish the fabric of time were light and transparent, that it came in sheets that I could roll up at will and tuck away out of sight behind a pile of books, only to be taken out when I feel like it. But what the past does to me is nail the years to my ribs so that they clad and cage me in a vicarious body, making my father's shadow loom large each time I furrow my brow, and my mother beat her arms like wings and hop in the air at each peal of my laughter, in which I can hear the echo of hers.

Who knows how many splinters of individuals whose names I've never heard of reside within my body? How many people am I unconsciously imitating in the way I sit on a chair, lift my glass, try to hide my impatience, snore in my sleep, press my lips together when I think, or put my hand to my chest when I listen? I see my great-grandfather, who died before I was born, making exactly the same gesture.

I did not set foot in my old room, although the door was wide open – Aunt had left it open for years to prevent things getting musty inside. Everything looked the same as in the beginning: the bed, the writing table, the grass-green bedspread, although the photo of Kennedy, still up on the mantelpiece, was very faded. There was no trace of the room having been occupied by me. If I had looked in the bottom of the wardrobe, I suppose I might have found the binoculars I used to point at the full moon in the hope of identifying the Sea of Tranquillity. So much the better for the antique dealer.

One day, when Uncle was still alive but already having difficulty walking, Aunt asked if I would fancy accompanying her to a film evening in the village. I did not dare say no.

The event was held in the parish hall. A crowd of pensioners milled about the projector. Aunt Laura beamed left and right, saying, 'Oh yes indeed, this is Joris – you know, George's boy.' Someone remarked that I was even taller than my father at my age.

'Stuyvenberghe of Old' was the title of the first film.

One of Mr Snellaert's sons was now in charge, the master having moved to a nursing home after a stroke. The father's hobby had evidently been passed on to the son.

He had made a compilation of the material his father had shot in the old days, although some sequences must have been even older. Films in which blobs of white or black appeared periodically beside the flying buttresses of the church, then still in possession of the pointed spire that was blown up by the Germans in the war. Jerky images of children trudging down the cobbled high street in wooden clogs lined with straw for warmth, dogcarts laden with milk churns, smiths at their anvils, country fairs, pilgrimages, and then all at once, in the rich Technicolor of the fifties, wheatfields with peasants tying the ears into sheaves and bundling the hay. Silent films, to which the master's son had added a soundtrack of schmaltzy German songs.

Next came 'Panoramic View from the Dike'. Violin glissandos skimmed the surface of the canal. The master had evidently turned in a full circle, sweeping the lens across fields, meadows, banks of brushwood and lines of poplars, then across the water, the village beyond, the tower, and yet more fields, as if to say: all this is about to get the chop.

I used to believe my father persuaded my mother to take so many photos of him and me together as a way of forestalling his misfortune, perhaps because he sensed that his days on this sublunary stage were numbered and that he needed to leave evidence for me when I grew up. The pictures he took of me, in my cradle, with my building blocks, in the back garden, under the apple trees, gave me a sense of his already being in some distant future, peering down at me through a chink in his afterlife.

I think he took to drink for the promise it held of other dimensions besides the four he already knew, for the euphoria of escape from the here and now, the straitjacket of stiffening joints, hardening arteries and diminishing opportunities.

During that film evening with Aunt I recall feeling embarrassed by her utter absorption in the show, which caused her to hum along with the soundtrack and sway her head from side to side in blissful affirmation, especially when the tree-lined alleyway to the manor came into view. I never told her what the girl had said about my father that afternoon at Hélène's coffee party.

I did drop some hints to my mother. On one of these occasions she burst out with 'He was on the bottle even before we were married . . . How can you think I had an easy time? I was barely out of my teens, for Christ's sake.'

I needed to grow quite a bit older before I could bring myself to take her in my arms, and even then I didn't mean it, I must confess, but on the other hand perhaps I meant it more than most. My own private history has its share of dark passages, which I tend to skip when browsing in the past, although my reaction to other people's obfuscations has always been to demand explanations, clarity, some kind of holdfast, and then to break with them in despair — and insist they return all my letters.

*

Aunt gave me a nudge in the ribs. 'Look, Joris!' she cried, overcome with delight.

I could see the path leading to the church and the leafy crowns of the lindens on either side. An early Sunday morning in summer. The door is open, the service has just ended. The first worshippers to depart appear at the threshold, farmers donning their caps and lingering for a chat. Hands are shaken, more people emerge from the church, the forecourt fills.

Aunt comes into view, wearing her Sunday coat. She stops to talk to a few women I don't recognise. Hélène Vuylsteke makes her appearance on the steps, holding the girl by the hand. Dispensing polite greetings left and right, they step briskly towards the high street, where their chauffeur is waiting at the kerb. Before getting into the car Hélène twists round to wave at Miss van Vooren, who has just emerged from the church beside the priest, clasping her missal with both hands.

It must have been during that final summer, some time after the fair, mid-July perhaps. The ruddy glow of the brick boundary wall, the colours of gravestones, linden leaves, garments, hair, hats – they all look so much richer than the way I remember them that summer.

But it was none of these things that moved Aunt to nudge me in the ribs. Her excitement was caused by a figure suddenly dashing across the screen from left to right, and then reappearing in a flash, like a swallow swooping over a country lane.

I had not noticed it was me until Aunt cried 'Look!' for

the second time. I am chasing my classmates, or they are chasing me. I snatch caps off boys' heads, dodge their grasping hands, stumble, regain my balance, swerve around groups of chatting villagers, vanish. A second or two later I am racing over the cobbles in the opposite direction.

Uncle tries to slow me down, I see him remonstrating with me, but I don't seem able to stop. I fling a cap in the air, evidently not mine because a boy with ginger hair lunges forward to catch it, but I jump and swipe it away. I see myself yelling voicelessly. I do not remember the words I shouted any more than I remember the happy, high-spirited boy leaping nimbly over cobbles and grave-stones with his shirt tails flapping out of his trousers.

IN THE END I SETTLED FOR THE SECOND MOST EXPENSIVE coffin, mainly because the undertaker's snootiness got on my nerves and I wanted to be done with it. The nine-thirty service – the least expensive option for a change – was attended by no more than a dozen mourners. A tremulous requiem rose from the throats of four old biddies in the choir. The priest hurried through the rites with a voice that seemed to issue from a drainpipe, and during his sermon confused Aunt's name with that of the deceased due to be consigned to the earth an hour later.

It was February, not the jolliest of months in which to die. Beyond the cypresses enclosing the graveyard I glimpsed the manor, its windows all shuttered and the beeches spreading leaflessly on either side. In previous years I had heard that the house was mostly unoccupied, except for a few weeks in summer and the occasional weekend during the hunting season.

'That hussy', as Aunt always referred to the girl, had in the meantime become engaged, perhaps to one of the posh young men dancing attendance on her one evening in the foyer of a Brussels theatre. It was the only time I'd set eyes on her since I left the village, and I was holding a glass of white wine in each hand as I made my way to the bench where my mother was waiting for me, no doubt gauging whether I was sufficiently at ease in what she called 'the world'.

Isabella Van Callant. She must have been about eighteen at the time. She wore her jet black hair in a thick pony tail threaded with strands of glitter, and laughed uproariously each time one of her admirers leaned over to whisper some little joke in her ear. I thought she was showing off.

She did not recognise me. Our eyes met, and she fixed me for a moment or two, during which a light frown spread across her forehead. Perhaps the sight of me tripped some vague recognition, perhaps I was just staring at her too openly.

She turned away. Her low-cut dress exposed a back and shoulder-blades dotted with moles.

'T'es maigre comme un clou,' I said to myself.

I stayed at the graveside until the workmen were ready to heave the slab in place. When Uncle Werner died Aunt had ordered her name to be chiselled into the bluestone in addition to his, and her date of birth followed by a dash, which could now be complemented by the date of her death.

Since then the concession has been extended twice already. Eternity seems to be less and less durable these days. On both occasions I hesitated by the reception area in the council office, thinking how absurd it was that even the dead were charged for bed and board despite a leaky roof and mould-infested walls, but both times I signed my name at the bottom of the form and paid the dues. That burial vault is a millstone round my neck, or an anchor, or a stake in the ground to which I am chained like a sheep in a field, and I cherish my chain.

The grave resembles a king-size double bed, notwithstanding its triple occupancy. On the mattress lies a crucifix of polished black granite. Aunt resides on the left-hand side, and on the right, roughly at Uncle Werner's feet, rests my father, considerably smaller in death than his twin brother, although the reverse was true in life. I picture them sometimes, crumpling up with laughter on the shared, heaving mattress, like children staying over at a friend's house.

The monstrosity was paid for by my mother, so I learned later. Even now, when I stand at the foot of that grotesque cradle of death, I have a feeling that they were somehow let down, done down, done away with, no doubt for my own good.

The anger welling up each time I stand there is not directed at them, but subconsciously at my mother. My mother, who enabled me to attend the best schools, to travel as much as I pleased and to take my pick from the pert middle-class girls she presented to me like strongly scented bouquets.

I suppose I paid her back by adopting the role of obnoxious teenager. The moment I realised this all the resentment fell away, and I was left merely with a person in her late fifties who dyed her hair the wrong colour and wore oversized earrings, a woman who had no connection whatsoever with the beautiful, dark-haired young mother looking down at the small boy hugging her shins as he watches the ducks in some pond.

The grandchildren she hoped would some day arrive never came. I would have made a far too posthumous sort of father.

I was taken ill that Friday evening in September when I returned to Stuyvenberghe after my first fortnight at the Jesuit school. I still take the same trip now and then, just to feel the city leaching from my shoulders as the train rumbles across the River Leie.

I had felt a hot swelling in my throat all week, on top of which came a splitting headache in the last couple of days. When I swallowed I could hear my eardrums creak. I felt bruised all over like a fruit about to burst with fermenting pulp.

When the train left the last suburbs behind and started across the river, I propped my elbows on the table beneath the window and pressed hard, as though moving my bowels. Release took minutes to arrive, racking my midriff like birth pangs until it all came out in waves.

I felt myself gushing out of my body and turning into someone else in the same compartment, someone with a stricken look, watching the tears run down the face of the child sitting opposite with his cap on and his travelling-bag between his feet, suffocating in a sadness both harrowing and brief.

I heard my own sobs reverberate against the wood cladding of the compartment. I heard the rails thrum beneath the wheels, rumble in my midriff. Through the window I saw vegetable plots, garden sheds and alder bushes flash past in the twilight of a day that had known little sunshine. It was around seven, the evening rush hour was over. There was no one in the compartment besides me.

We sat there like brothers, or like sweethearts who haven't dared to tell their parents yet, forehead to forehead, mouth to mouth. I felt the tears trickling down my hands into my sleeves and my cap sliding off my head and on to the table.

Someone slid the door open. The ticket inspector rapped his punch against the metal surround and said good evening. While I hunted frantically in my pockets he whistled a jaunty tune. Perhaps he was new at the job. When he handed me my ticket back I wanted to crawl under the bench out of mortification.

I pulled myself together, dried my cheeks with my handkerchief, folded my arms and leaned forward on the table. I tried to count the far-off church towers, but in the gathering dusk it was increasingly hard to avoid seeing my face reflected in the glass.

★

In the blue evening haze, the village roofs were settling in around the church like lambs in the fold, under a huge sky balancing precariously on the bell tower. I could hear the high-tension cables hum as the train gathered speed on its way to the horizon.

The cafés on the station square had already lowered their blinds. A cat ambled along the edge of the pavement. From some buildings wafted the sound of the evening news; elsewhere spoons clattered in saucepans.

Past the rectory garden I turned left to strike across the churchyard as usual, but I came upon a metal barrier behind which a tent of grey plastic sheeting had been erected. Red-and-white strips had been tied between the lindens, one of which had a sign nailed to its trunk saying WORKS EXIT. Muddy tyre tracks fanned out on the asphalt of the high street.

I had to take the long way home, past my old school and past Miss van Vooren's house, which was engulfed in the shadow of the cedars that would, in years to come, press against its walls like fingers. I was shivering with fever, my cheeks were on fire.

Dogs began to bark in the back gardens on the other side of the hedges lining the church lane. Worm-eaten apples hung from the branches among the last remaining leaves. I felt my weekend bag scraping against my ankle. The fever engulfed me in waves of Saharan heat.

It had started to drizzle. All around me the smell of long-parched earth yearning for rain floated up from the cracks in the pavement.

On the near side of the church, against the north transept, the graveyard had not yet been cordoned off. The gravestones stood erect, shoulder to shoulder, like a row of house-fronts in the greenish ground that rarely got any sun, but on the far side, over the brick wall, more barriers and tents awaited me. The shop looked out on a mass of plastic sheeting. Against the wall by the choir lay the nozzle of a hose, agape like the maw of a prehistoric beast.

I pushed open the door as Aunt was serving her last customer, who glanced over his shoulder to see who had come in. I heard him say, 'Well now, here's the student.' The handle of my bag slipped from my grasp.

'Gracious, lad,' cried Aunt, 'whatever's the matter with you?'

'Nothing, it's nothing,' I replied, but I couldn't stop shaking.

'Children,' said the customer, 'a never-ending worry, eh?'

I couldn't put one foot ahead of another, so over-powered was I by the aromas coming my way like the old familiar faces of elderly relatives approaching in carpet slippers.

The smell of peppermint, freshly roasted coffee, smoked ham, snuff tobacco. The smell of cinnamon, of wild thyme, and the primness of the lavender sachets piled up at the far end of one of the shelves, waiting to suffuse every wardrobe with moth-free eternity. My ears were tweaked, I was tapped under my chin, I heard whispers. I saw the tins swell up on the shelves, I could hear their contents slop like digestive tracts. Beneath my feet the floor appeared to tilt and sway.

A cramp in my midriff doubled me up and prised open my jaws. I began to retch.

'Good Lord,' cried Aunt, rushing out from behind the counter with her apron held out in front of her. 'Not on my floor! I only just mopped it!'

I pushed her away. 'It's nothing, I'm all right again now.'

'Hurry up inside, then,' she said, drawing herself up. 'Werner!'

At the end of the passage I saw Uncle rise to his feet in the yellowish light of the reading lamp, beneath which he had no doubt been engrossed in the paper.

He turned and saw me. 'Oh my poor boy, poor poor boy . . .'

He held out his arms. I sucked my lungs full of air to stave off a fresh wave of nausea, broke into a run as if my life depended on it, and hurled myself into his embrace. It was more of a head-on collision than a hug.

I can recall the rest of that evening in the minutest detail. During the intervals when the fever abated somewhat and a rush of coolness buffeted my bones, I was overwhelmed by a sensation of clarity no less beguiling than a mirage. The tureen filled with steaming broth, the dark brown loaf on the breadboard, the thick slices of macerated meat Aunt dished out, the wine-red checks on my sleeves. I was wearing Uncle's dressing gown, which he had made me put on when he rinsed out my vomit-soiled shirt in the kitchen.

Outside, the Virginia creeper became tinged with mauve in the fading light, until the leaves were absorbed into the darkness of the garden. I heard Aunt saying they had no right to put me on a train by myself in the state I was in, and Uncle responding with a soothing 'Now then, Ma', to make her stop grumbling.

She had given me an aspirin. I sucked the pink tablet as judiciously as I could in order to prolong the bitterness on my palate and luxuriate in my invalid status. I don't know if it was in fact influenza that had felled me. The preceding weeks had been harrowing. The city had swallowed me up in a chaos of honking vehicles, tram-cars jangling down streets on the end of electric tethers, office blocks periodically disgorging workers, esplanades inundated by civil servants waiting to be scooped up by water wheels of buses.

And then there was the playground with its colonnaded perimeter, where robed figures glided over the tiled walk as if they were airborne, where the hands of the clock reigned supreme, ruling lessons and breaks, causing bells to ring, sirens to go off, and stairs to shake under the recurrent stampede of feet on their way to the classroom or gymnasium.

Aunt made me comfortable in the armchair by the stove where she always sat when it grew chilly in the house. I remember how debilitated I felt as I nestled myself against the back of the chair in the luxury of the oversized dressing gown and a pair of Norwegian woolly socks, likewise oversized, as if I were retreating into a shell which, although it felt too big for me, would shortly prove too stifling, too starved of oxygen.

For despite the pain of those first weeks away from home, despite the cool and mechanical welcome afforded by my new environment, a world bereft of grass growing between cobbles and languorous afternoons to be whiled away at will, my imagination had been fired: as I marched down the school corridors that reeked of floor polish I could not take my eyes off the succession of maps lining the walls.

Snuggling down further into the armchair I listened to the music of the house, the slap of Aunt's playing cards on the tabletop, Uncle crinkling his newspaper into labyrinthine folds for supposed ease of reading. The unpretentious symphony of familiarity, with that far-off door that would not stop banging, the leaky tap in the kitchen pattering a paternoster into the sink, the wind gusting down the chimney and the slightly out-of-kilter storage unit halfway down the passage, which always gave a loud indignant grunt when its doors were yanked open.

After the clock struck ten, Uncle asked whether I wanted him to carry me upstairs.

'Oh please, don't exaggerate,' I said gruffly, and the hoarseness in my throat persisted in the following weeks until the last trace of my boy's voice had been abraded out of existence.

From my bedroom window I could just see over the barrier. I could make out the shapes of the gravestones. Some of the crosses sagged, huddling together like lambs.

I saw a giant shovel, the outstretched arm of a crane. It was as if the subsoil had melted during the day, as if the stones had slipped from their moorings and would now drift this way and that on the surface until the cold of evening froze the ground again.

Fingernails of rain tapped against the window pane. A breeze played in the tarpaulins, making them reflect the silver-white shimmer of the street lamp.

I took off the dressing gown and crept under the icy covers. Not three weeks had passed since my departure, but the wall beside the bed already gave off the brackish smell of abandoned buildings.

I sank into a slumber that felt like a body of water closing overhead. In the course of the night the fever raised me periodically to the surface, where I bathed in sweat. I turned over on my side and curled up, hugging my knees to my chest. I tumbled down snow-covered slopes, rolled through savannahs, dreamed of forests where the only sounds were birdsong and raindrops splattering on the foliage. All my tossing and turning had stencilled the sheets with an assortment of sweaty contours, so that I seemed to be lying back to back with myself.

Lianas twisted themselves about my ankles. I started awake from their stranglehold and got out of bed to fetch a glass of water. My sweat-drenched vest was a cold harness encasing my ribcage.

I stole through the darkened house to the scullery. All I longed for was to let go, topple over backwards, and heave a succession of sighs so that I might at length be subsumed into the plaster on the walls.

I held the glass under the tap, downed it in two, three draughts, filled it again, and again, and yet again, until the rawness in my throat had passed.

I don't know what time it was, but it must have been close to midday, for broth being prepared in the kitchen could be smelt all over the house. Saturday – miserable weather and cups of hot broth.

I was lying on my back. I must have slept with my mouth open because my palate felt like sandpaper when I swallowed.

Sitting up at last I felt the sodden state of my sheets and realised I had wet myself. I leaped out of bed, swearing under my breath. I stripped off my underwear, put on the dressing gown and went to the bathroom with my vest and pants tucked under my arm.

I stood in the tub to have a wash, not daring to glance at my reflection in the mirror over the basin. After towelling myself dry, I rinsed out the underwear, shivering from cold and from the trickles of yellow on my fingers. It was all in vain, of course. When Aunt came upstairs later to make the beds she certainly noticed the state of my sheets. I cringed with embarrassment.

I threw the damp underclothes in the laundry basket on the landing, and when I was back in my room putting on a clean vest I heard something outside: a metallic scraping noise from across the road.

I squeezed between my writing table and my bed to get to the window and pushed the net curtain aside.

Raindrops slithered over the panes. The plastic sheeting across the road sagged in places from the weight of the collected rainwater.

I could see Uncle Werner talking to the priest, who held one hand to his head to stop the rising wind from whipping off his hat. Both of them were looking down at a third person, of whom I caught only the occasional glimpse: a bent back, a cap, an elbow, a hand gripping the handle of a spade or some other implement.

The wind tore at the long mackintosh the priest wore over his cassock. At one point I saw Uncle looking the other way, perhaps to avoid the lashing rain. He gazed out over the churchyard stretching out before him like a cratered, lunar landscape, which looked as if some giant marmot or mole had been burrowing into the ground to excavate a series of tunnels.

The priest nodded in response to something Uncle said. The third figure drew himself upright. I recognised him as a local man who was employed by the public works department. He stood with muddied hands beside Uncle and the priest, all three of them with their heads down, staring at something at their feet. Then the workman bent over again. The priest turned to Uncle Werner and spoke a few words.

The rain intensified. I saw them confer about taking shelter from the downpour. The man appeared to be lifting something. The three men moved towards the road, where they were screened from view by the plastic sheeting.

I was on the landing, poised to start down the stairs when I heard them come in. Boots were stamped on the doorstep.

'We might as well wait for them here,' I heard Uncle say. 'Better than drowning under a tree . . .'

They were pushing and shoving some heavy object.

'Yes, leave it here. That's all right . . . we're closed anyway.'

I heard them go down the passage to the kitchen. I buttoned up Uncle's dressing gown and went downstairs.

'Anyone for some good hot broth?' Aunt called from the range. 'Or something stronger, perhaps . . . or would you prefer a cup of coffee?'

When I came down all four of them were sitting around the table. The workman added a dash of genever to his coffee. The priest knocked back a thimble-sized glass of liquor and breathed out through clenched teeth. They had not noticed me yet.

'So you see,' said the priest, 'some things are best left undisturbed . . .'

I saw Uncle Werner nod in agreement.

'Ha!' cried Aunt. 'He's awake. You look a sight better already. Can I get you something to eat, lad?'

I shook my head. 'Don't think so. Wouldn't keep it down anyway.'

'Bearing up all right over at the Jesuits?' asked the priest. 'Not the gentlest of folks by all accounts, eh?'

I shrugged my shoulders. 'Not bad.' Then I felt compelled to say I was sorry about the canopy, last summer.

'Not to worry,' he said, laughing indulgently. 'Just a

little accident, that's all . . . ' He turned to face the company again.

'It's a funny business, though,' I heard the workman say. 'Not that I haven't seen my share. Remember Richard, the old gamekeeper? Yesterday, it was. And the little girl, daughter of the baker's brother-in-law . . . All look the same in the end . . .'

Aunt laid her hand on his arm. 'Are you sure you don't want some of my nice broth? Shame to let it go cold. Come on, folks, have a taste.'

She stood up and went through to the scullery.

I left the men behind and lurked in the passage.

My father. It must have been close on ten years since I had last set eyes on him. Ten years in which it was not he who tossed me in the air, nor he who took me by the hand and showed me the way along paths I have since learned to walk unaided, despite the worsening bumps and potholes in the surface under my feet.

He stood on the mat in the doorway, looking as forlorn as a prodigal son seeking refuge from the wind and the rain. Behind him, in the porch, stood a pair of muddy boots and a spade, as if he had dug a tunnel from the other side of the globe just to be here.

I heard a faint echo of his laughter, his voice, his intonations, the expressions he used, the gist of which eluded me as it had in the old days. I was not yet thirteen, but he barely reached to my calves.

I heard Aunt calling my name, and then, more quietly,

addressing the men in the kitchen: 'Where can he have got to?'

I looked down at the dark, mahogany box. She had bought him a handsome new trunk, had my mother, not much bigger than a suitcase.

I bent down, rubbed my thumbs over his shoulders of stained wood, ran my fingers over the braille of the plaque on the lid and felt the coolness of the brass handles on either side.

I heard a rushing sound, as if all the photos ever taken of him were suddenly rising from their albums and boxes and picture frames, as if he had let go of my hand to startle the butterflies that had hovered motionless over the hemlock ever since. But like as not it was only my head spinning faster and faster as I sank to my knees and laid my feverish cheek against the wood.

The dressing gown hampered me, so I untied the belt. I clenched my fingers around the handles. The box was lighter than I expected. Just as it rose up from the doorstep something came loose inside, rolled over the base and bumped hollowly against the back, followed by a dry rattle like jostling marbles.

The sound pierced me to the quick. I let go of the handles.

'Joris?' I heard Aunt cry.

I ran past her down the passage and up the stairs.

In my room I stripped my mattress, bundled up my sheets, threw them on the floor, kicked them under my bed. I drew the curtains to darken the room. The rain had lifted to a drizzle.

I sat down on the bare mattress in the sepia light filtering through the curtains. I don't know how long I sat there.

A car pulled up on the cobbles. Someone got out, the engine was still running. The shop's bell tinkled.

'Anybody in?' someone called. And I heard Aunt reply: 'Yes, yes, over here.'

'Can I ride with you?' I heard a voice ask — the priest's, by the sound of it.

The bell tinkled again.

'I'll join you later . . .' Uncle called.

I got to my feet, crossed to the window, draped the curtain around my shoulders and stood with my fingers pressing on the wood of the sill, which was softened by age and sudden showers and seemed to be held in place by nothing but coats of paint.

I glimpsed a figure in a dark suit shutting the back of the hearse, and then I saw the priest getting in next to the driver.

Car doors thudded. They drove off. A while later Uncle hove into view, riding his bicycle down the path.

I turned round, let the curtains fall in folds over my head, went back to the bed and stubbed my toe against the table leg on the way.

I stood on one leg and swore, holding my aching foot in the air.

All I wanted was to stop moving, to just stand there

and turn to stone, even if I knew I looked stupid in my uncle's flowing dressing gown with only a cotton vest underneath. In the commotion that morning I had forgotten to put on a clean pair of underpants.

There was a knock at the door.

Aunt said my name.

I kept silent.

'Joris?' she repeated.

I turned my back to the door and went to the window, where the glow of sunbeams suddenly breaking through the clouds lit up the weave of the curtain fabric.

'Why don't you say something, lad?' She sounded fraught. Twisting the doorknob she said, 'You're not doing anything silly, are you?'

'It's all wet . . .' I heard myself say in a small voice. 'I've wet my bed.'

She let go of the doorknob.

I heard a sigh.

'You poor thing. Never mind, it doesn't matter. Come on, please open the door,' she pleaded softly.

I turned the key, but first I buttoned up the dressing gown.

She entered, took my head in her hands and pulled me towards her.

I did not resist.

'These things happen,' she murmured in my ear, 'what must out, must out . . .'

THE WORLD OF YESTERDAY
STEFAN ZWEIG

'*The World of Yesterday* is one of the greatest memoirs of the twentieth century, as perfect in its evocation of the world Zweig loved, as it is in its portrayal of how that world was destroyed' David Hare

JOURNEY BY MOONLIGHT
ANTAL SZERB

'Just divine… makes you imagine the author has had private access to your own soul' Nicholas Lezard, *Guardian*

BONITA AVENUE
PETER BUWALDA

'One wild ride: a swirling helix of a family saga… a new writer as toe-curling as early Roth, as roomy as Franzen and as caustic as Houellebecq' *Sunday Telegraph*

THE PARROTS
FILIPPO BOLOGNA

'A five-star satire on literary vanity… a wonderful, surprising novel' *Metro*

I WAS JACK MORTIMER
ALEXANDER LERNET-HOLENIA

'Terrific… a truly clever, rather wonderful book that both plays with and defies genre' Eileen Battersby, *Irish Times*

SONG FOR AN APPROACHING STORM
PETER FRÖBERG IDLING

'Beautifully evocative… a must-read novel' *Daily Mail*

THE RABBIT BACK LITERATURE SOCIETY
PASI ILMARI JÄÄSKELÄINEN

'Wonderfully knotty… a very grown-up fantasy masquerading as quirky fable. Unexpected, thrilling and absurd' *Sunday Telegraph*

RED LOVE: THE STORY OF AN EAST GERMAN FAMILY
MAXIM LEO

'Beautiful and supremely touching… an unbearably poignant description of a world that no longer exists' *Sunday Telegraph*

THE BREAK

PIETRO GROSSI

'Small and perfectly formed… reaching its end leaves the reader desirous to start all over again' *Independent*

FROM THE FATHERLAND, WITH LOVE

RYU MURAKAMI

'If Haruki is *The Beatles* of Japanese literature, Ryu is its *Rolling Stones*' David Pilling

BUTTERFLIES IN NOVEMBER

AUÐUR AVA ÓLAFSDÓTTIR

'A funny, moving and occasionally bizarre exploration of life's upheavals and reversals' *Financial Times*

BARCELONA SHADOWS

MARC PASTOR

'As gruesome as it is gripping… the writing is extraordinarily vivid… Highly recommended' *Independent*

THE LAST DAYS

LAURENT SEKSIK

'Mesmerising… Seksik's portrait of Zweig's final months is dignified and tender' *Financial Times*

BY BLOOD

ELLEN ULLMAN

'Delicious and intriguing' *Daily Telegraph*

WHILE THE GODS WERE SLEEPING

ERWIN MORTIER

'A monumental, phenomenal book' *De Morgen*

THE BRETHREN

ROBERT MERLE

'A master of the historical novel' *Guardian*